Murder On Old Main Street

Halfway back up the stairs with the filled pitcher, I heard the distinctive sound of the light switch in Jimmy's office clicking off. The space above me went dark, and I froze where I stood. For fully thirty seconds I stood stock still, every sense straining to come up with some logical reason why I had heard what I heard and seen what I'd seen. Only one presented itself. I did not want to accept it, but ultimately, I had no choice. For who knows how long, someone else had been in the Law Barn with me, someone who did not want me to see him.

Unless I was very much mistaken, I had just taken elaborate pains to lock myself in with Prudy Crane's murderer.

Other Works From The Pen Of
Judith K. Ivie

Waiting for Armando

While waiting for her longtime love interest to return from South America, feisty Kate Lawrence and friends scramble to exonerate a colleague accused of murdering a partner at their prominent Connecticut law firm.

Don't Say Goodbye To Love

Faced with the possibility of losing a loved one, newly separated Jennie and Carl are helped by their family and friends to put pride aside and rediscover their true feelings in this Christmas-in-New England romance.

Wings

Murder On Old Main Street

A Murder New England Style Mystery

by

Judith K. Ivie

A Wings ePress, Inc.

Mystery Novel

Wings ePress, Inc.

Edited by: Dianne Hamilton
Copy Edited by: Sara V. Olds
Senior Editor: Dianne Hamilton
Managing Editor: Leslie Hodges
Executive Editor: Lorraine Stephens
Cover Artist: Pat Casey

All rights reserved

Names, characters and incidents depicted in this book are products of the author's imagination or are used fictitiously. Any resemblance to actual events, locales, organizations, or persons, living or dead, is entirely coincidental and beyond the intent of the author or the publisher.

No part of this book may be reproduced or transmitted in any form or by any means, electronic or mechanical, including photocopying, recording, or by any information storage and retrieval system, without permission in writing from the publisher.

Wings ePress Books
http://www.wings-press.com

Copyright © 2007 by Judith K. Ivie
ISBN 918-1-59705-877-3

Published In the United States Of America

October 2007

Wings ePress Inc.
403 Wallace Court
Richmond, KY 40475

Dedication

To Laura, Ed, Jay, Emily, and all the others who make Blades such a joy to patronize… to Janice, Angie, Sherri and everyone else at the Town Line Diner, who make weekend breakfast so much fun… and to "Emma," "Joey" and "Manny": the lights of my life.

Explanations and Acknowledgments

I have no fear that residents of Old Wethersfield will mistake my fictitious portrait of our town for the real thing, and those who live elsewhere won't be troubled. Still, there are enough similarities to warrant an explanation, so here it is: While I have appropriated the geography of Wethersfield's Historic District, *Murder on Old Main Street* is entirely a work of fiction. No character is based on a real individual, whether living or dead, known to me or unknown, and any likeness to a real individual is entirely coincidental.

Further, while I have shamelessly mentioned by name some of my favorite landmarks and business establishments along Old Main Street and elsewhere in Wethersfield, I have created others simply to facilitate the story.

Those of you who are familiar with the structure formerly known as the *Law Barn* may be disappointed to learn that the back story I've provided about it is also pure fiction. Sorry, but there is no secret room, to my knowledge. I did run across something like it years ago in an old brownstone on Beacon Street in Boston. The building had been turned into a rooming house, and a friend who rented space on the first floor showed me a hidden door in the parlor paneling that opened into a tiny powder room. I was enchanted with the idea of a hidey-hole, and the memory stuck with me.

I am most grateful to my daughter, Jennafer Sprankle, for her help with the details of real estate transactions, as well as for her advice throughout the writing of *Murder on Old Main Street.* Thanks for the crash course, Dearie.

Chief James Cetran of the Wethersfield Police was extraordinarily generous with his time while setting me straight on the department's investigative procedures, as was Chief Thomas Sweeney of the Glastonbury Police Department. Gentlemen, I am indebted to you both and hope I have portrayed both departments with the respect and accuracy they deserve.

Judith K. Ivie
March, 2007

One

It's not that I don't understand why people smoke. I do. I myself enjoyed cigarettes for some twenty years, on and off. The "off" part was during the two pregnancies that had produced my son Joey and daughter Emma, so obviously, I always knew that smoking was an unhealthy indulgence. But it took the sudden and untimely deaths of my father and mother, both lifelong smokers, to get me to lay that lighter down for good.

First Dad, a pack-a-day man since World War II, suffered a massive coronary at the age of 63. After lunch one day, he just fell to the floor of the warehouse he managed, and the paramedics abandoned their attempts to resuscitate him after half an hour. A few years later, Mother's heart gave out as she was clearing snow from the sidewalk in front of the house where I grew up. The exertion triggered the attack, said the nice young resident whose job it had been to break the news that Mother hadn't survived emergency surgery, but the real damage had been done over the previous decades, one cigarette at a time.

"That's what people your mom's age can't seem to get," he said sadly. "Every time she lit a cigarette, she was holding a gun to her head. It just takes longer for the bullet to kill you."

My decision to stop wasn't a conscious one. I simply holstered my lighter and never had another cigarette after that day. My habit had been moderate. I had smoked only half a dozen cigarettes a day, so quitting wasn't really a big deal. I was one of the lucky ones who hadn't become physically or psychologically addicted, which made it all the more incomprehensible that I had ever taken it up. But I did, and then I lost my parents, and then I stopped. End of story, right?

Fast forward seventeen years. It's a new millennium, and the war between smokers and nonsmokers is in full spate. There's no avoiding the issue; you have to choose a side. Because of the overlapping rights of both groups, there's no middle ground to occupy, no way to live and let live. The obese woman shoveling down a banana split at the next table is endangering only her health, not yours, so it's her life, her choice. The smoker who's dangling his Marlborough out the window of the car in front of you is a different story, however. It's his choice to inhale the deadly toxins, but the secondhand smoke he huffs out the window pollutes your air almost as lethally. His rights have to end where yours begin. That was at least part of the reason underlying the local business association's recent proposal. Smoking inside eating establishments was already prohibited by law throughout Connecticut. The business association now proposed to ban smoking anywhere in the historic district of Old Wethersfield, indoors or out, as of October fifteenth.

"Why do smokers do that anyway?" choked my partner Margo, waving away the fumes emanating from the Bronco idling in front of us at the light.

I had collected Margo and her constant companion, a chocolate Labrador retriever named Rhett Butler, at the dealership where her ancient BMW had been left for servicing. Rhett accompanied Margo nearly everywhere, asking nothing more than to be allowed to walk adoringly by her side. He had been enjoying the morning breeze through an open window, but now Margo raised it. He whined in protest and flopped full-length across my back seat, which meant he took up all of it.

"I know, Sugar, but what can I do?" Margo told him. "If that silly Yankee wants to smell disgustin', let him roll up his windows and keep the smoke all to himself, but I just had this suit dry-cleaned, thank you."

I could understand Margo's concern. The understated Donna Karan in shades of taupe and black set off her southern belle good looks to a fare-thee-well. Definitely worth not stinking up. I, on the other hand, could safely drop my easy-care Susan Gravers into the washer and dryer.

I'm Kate Lawrence… well, Sarah Katherine Lawrence, actually, but who wants to go through life tagged as an Ivy League institution? Margo Farnsworth is one of my business partners, as well as my dearest friend, and we were on our way to work on a crisp, late September Monday. In the year since we had opened our new real estate brokerage in historic Wethersfield Village where we shared office space with my daughter Emma and her lawyer boss in a renovated barn on Old Main Street, business had grown steadily. It hadn't been easy, but we hadn't expected it to be, and the problems had been far outweighed by the excitement of launching a business of our own. That was the point, after all: to create something that was our own.

The temporary absence this month of our third partner, Charlene "Strutter" Tuttle, was a small setback. In a classic case of bad timing, from Margo's and my perspective anyway, the Jamaican beauty had fallen madly in love with a mortgage broker who turned out to be wooing more than our referral business, but hey, what are you going to do? She and her young son Charlie deserved a good man like John Putnam in their lives, and things at the office would get back to normal as soon as they returned from their extended honeymoon.

Fortunately, the real estate market was red hot, and business was booming. Margo and Strutter had been on the road from one end of the day to the other, checking out new listings, showing properties, and holding open houses for the slow movers on weekends. For my part, it was all I could do to keep up with the phone, which rang constantly. I also managed all the sale documents, the preparation of which I was happy to hand off to Emma and her boss, real estate lawyer Jimmy Seidel, and coped with the myriad administrative details that were part and parcel of running any business.

Emma and Jimmy occupied the *Law Barn*'s loft area along with another young lawyer, Donatella Puccini, and two more paralegals. More often than not, Jimmy or "Pooch" represented our clients at the closings, and Emma and her assistants shepherded them through the maze of pre-closing paperwork. The entrance area of the building was presided over by pretty Jenny Morris, a law student by night and our receptionist by day. Jenny answered all of our phones, took prodigious messages, placated nervous clients, and somehow managed to get everything properly filed before dashing off to her evening classes.

The remaining *Law Barn* office was occupied by Millicent Haines, a middle-aged mortgage broker who had rented the small, first-floor room off the area where our copier and fax machine were housed. Having relocated from California this past July, Millie spent most of her days on the phone or out of the office, so the noise of the machines didn't bother her. She seemed pleasant enough, on the few occasions our paths crossed, and the clients we referred to her for help with their financing seemed well pleased.

As hectic as our days were, it never occurred to us to complain. MACK Realty was ours—no more strutting, egotistical bosses to humor, as we had endured at the law firm where Margo, Strutter and I had been legal assistants until last summer. As Margo put it so well in the honeyed Georgia drawl that kept the northern fellows hanging on her every word, "No more arrogant, demanding bosses for us to placate, Sugar, not for us spirited, not to mention gorgeous, business women."

Strutter had concurred dryly, "Yessirree, it's nothing but arrogant, demanding clients to placate from now on!"

Things were going well for me on other fronts, too. Following a bumpy settling-in period, during which my neighbors and I had snarled regularly at each other as we chafed under the rules and regulations of condominium living, I was enjoying life in my spacious unit at The Birches. Situated on the acreage of one of Wethersfield's oldest farms, the freestanding Colonial homes were beautifully landscaped and backed by EPA protected woods and wetlands, which gave Jasmine and Simon, my feline housemates, plenty of visual entertainment from their sunny windowsills.

Perhaps best of all, things were going swimmingly with my longtime love interest, Armando Velasquez, so swimmingly, in fact, that we were considering what both of us had sworn never to consider again: sharing a roof. My roof, to be precise, since home for Manny was a one-bedroom efficiency in a pet-free building in West Hartford. But after luxuriating in our individual spaces for more than a decade following our respective, amicable divorces from our respective, amicable ex-spouses, cohabiting was not something to be entered into lightly. We weren't kids anymore, and while our attraction to each other was undeniable, we were no longer slaves to the hormones that had driven us at a younger age into marriage. Still, we had been going together for more than five years. Although the idea of marriage still made us both skittish, we were at least beginning to consider combining residences.

So I had plenty to think about on the way to work that morning. I drove down Welles Road and crossed the Silas Deane Highway, Wethersfield's commercial thoroughfare. A mere hundred yards farther along, a wooden sign pronounced quaintly that I was entering the Village of Wethersfield, "Ye Most Ancient Towne," established in

1633-34. One long curve to the left, and suburban Connecticut *circa* 2006 gave way to the New England ambience of earlier centuries. The 25 m.p.h. speed limit seemed entirely appropriate to the venerable elms and oaks shading stately homes, set well back and interspersed with more contemporary dwellings, on Old Main Street. As always, I enjoyed the transition, noting the spreading colors in the sumac of the hedges and the sugar maples. In late September, the school buses had been on the roads for several weeks already. The two family farm stands on the Broad Street Green were still open for business, but apples and mums had joined the late tomatoes and the last of the sweet corn offered for sale, and pumpkins would soon appear. A third farm around the corner was beginning to offer hayrides. It was my favorite time of year, since I was not fond of Connecticut's humid summers, but my enjoyment was bittersweet, knowing that the cold rains of November would soon be with us.

In a week, the Autumn Festival would be in full swing with local businesses and nonprofits awaiting the formal judging of the annual *Scarecrows Along Main Street* competition, in which entries could be almost anything, so long as they were at least partially constructed of straw. Up and down the length of Old Main Street, dozens of whimsical displays already adorned front yards and porches, with dozens more under construction. Some were perennial favorites, welcomed back as old friends, such as the overall-clad farmer holding a lapful of corn as he sat on a sunny bench outside the museum. Many were the work of first-timers, like this year's "Baby Broomers," a motley collection of brooms with faces propped against a white picket fence. The "Ghoul-Aid Stand" on the corner of Garden Street gave everyone who passed a chuckle. Old and new, we all enjoyed the collective creative effort.

I pulled the Altima into my favorite space just south of the *Law Barn*'s driveway. Margo checked her make-up in the visor mirror and winked at herself. "Sugar, nobody would take either one of us for a day over forty," she pronounced with satisfaction.

"Well," I demurred, "forty-two maybe…"

"…but a great forty-two!" we chorused, ending our standard gag.

I waved so long as Margo and Rhett disappeared into the building while I stayed in the car to wait for my daughter. At least twice a week, I met Emma before work, and we power-walked to the cove at the end of Old Main Street and back. The exercise cleared the cobwebs from our sleep-fogged heads. It also gave us a chance to catch up with each other's lives before the demands of the clients we shared crowded into the day. On the return leg of our walk, we stopped into the Village Diner for coffee to go, then sipped and chatted as we completed the circuit at a more leisurely pace.

I laced my feet into white Avias as I waited for Emma. Just thinking of her made me smile, as did the thought of my son Joey, who at the age of 28 was on the road seeing the country as a long-distance trucker. The tractor cab of his "reefer," which was trucker lingo for the refrigerated trailer he hauled, was better-appointed than most of his friends' apartments, and he was enjoying the adventure of his gypsy existence. Emma, at 27, preferred her snug loft apartment and job as a residential real estate paralegal, at which she excelled. Both my kids were bright, strong, and funny as hell, and I was proud of them both. Better yet, they seemed to like me, despite all of my parenting mistakes, and to seek out my company without inordinate prodding from me. The same went for their relationship with their father, who had remarried happily a few years back.

Life was good, I congratulated myself on this September morning. Promising shafts of sunlight pierced the low fog that rolled off the nearby Connecticut River, and it looked to be another glorious day. Despite the early hour, I noted a number of cars parked in front of other business establishments, whose owners were also attempting to get a jump on the day. As I waited, I admired the scarecrow in front of the *Law Barn*, which had been the brainchild of Emma and her colleagues. A stern-faced black crow in a judge's robe sat behind his bench made of hay bales. Before him stood a braying ass clad in a suit and tie fashioned entirely of writs, deeds, subpoenas, wills and other legal documents. An overflowing briefcase leaned against his left foreleg. The exhibit was entitled, "Lawsuit." Biased though I was, I thought it might just be a winner.

"Hey, Mamacita!" Emma greeted me, using the nickname she had assigned to me following a long-ago semester of high school Spanish. She flashed me a dazzling smile and U-turned in the empty street to pull her silver Saturn up to the bumper of the Altima. Her face was free of make-up, and she efficiently wound her long hair, which was the same shade of ash blonde as my own short mop, into a casual knot and secured it firmly to the top of her head before hopping out of the car. Within minutes, we were stumping past the small shops, bed-and-breakfasts, and private residences, most with a creative scarecrow out front that lined the street. "So give with the latest on you and the Colombian," she said, making reference to Manny's South American roots.

"We're talking," I huffed, struggling to keep pace with her younger legs, "but there are issues. We'll see."

Emma rolled her eyes at me. Her brown irises flecked with green were another of our shared traits. "By the time you two get through hashing out your issues, you'll be sharing a room at the old folks' home and driving the nurses crazy. It's been more than five years, 'Cita. Face it, you're stuck with each other."

"What you mean is, at this point, no one else would have either one of us?"

Emma prudently didn't comment. "Manny's got his kinks, but you're no walk in the park either. When you come right down to it, everybody has their little weirdnesses. You always told me that the only thing that matters in a relationship is that you can live with his kinks, and he can live with yours. So, do you think you can?"

"Hard to say," I commented tersely, trying to conserve my oxygen. "He likes the TV and music on all the time, and I like silence. He's a packrat, I'm neat." *Pant, pant.* "He sleeps late and stays up late, and I'm up at five thirty and in bed by ten." I stopped walking and put my foot up on a convenient bench, ostensibly to retie my shoelace. Emma wasn't fooled.

"Get moving, old woman," she said, steaming forward

mercilessly, "or no bagel with your coffee today." I groaned and trotted to catch up with her. "Besides, who's to say you can't make those differences work in your favor?"

I remained silent but raised an eyebrow questioningly.

"Think about it. You'll each have your own bedroom and bathroom, so you won't need to tiptoe around each other. When you get up at the crack of dawn, he'll still be tucked up. You can have your coffee and crossword puzzle in the silence you love, then hit the shower. When you're ready to leave the house, he'll just be getting up and can blast the *Today* show. At night, it's the reverse. You get to come home to an empty house and wind down in peace. He gets home from work at 8:00, warms up the extra plate of supper you've left in the microwave, you chat a little, and you're off to bed with a book while he does TV."

I considered Emma's scenario as we passed a row of business establishments on the opposite side of the street. The line-up included Antiques on Main, which sold a fascinating collection of antiques and furniture oddments; Blades Salon, where all the really good local gossip was exchanged while hair and skin and fingers and toes were whipped into shape; Mainly Tea, which served up luncheons and high teas to eager locals and tourists alike five days a week; and Heart of the Country, another lovely gift shop. Apparently, the salon and the antiques shop had collaborated on their scarecrow exhibit, which featured two ladies of advanced years, seated under old-fashioned dryers. Their hair was in rollers, and they sipped tea from lovely old cups. A third scarecrow presided over the bone china teapot and an antique cash register set atop a hay bale.

"What about weekends?" I demanded as we passed the Village Diner on the corner, unwilling to be so easily swayed. We would stop in on our way back to get coffee to bring to the office. Early morning patrons already sat at the counter and tables, hoping to be waited on soon by surly Prudence Crane, widely acknowledged to be the worse waitress in town. None of us could understand why Abigail Stoddard, who managed the diner, put up with her.

"Oh, get a grip! You're together all weekend now. What will be any different?"

She had a point. I trudged on mutely. Then, "How about the packrat versus neat freak thing?" Ha! I had her there, I thought, but Emma remained serene.

"He can get only so much stuff in his room, and if you can't stand the sight of it, do what you did with Joey and me when we were teenagers. Just close the door. Besides," she added, playing her ace, "there's Grace."

I had almost forgotten about Grace. By this time, we were on the outskirts of the Old Main Street business district and began to descend a small slope into the parking area for Wethersfield Cove. Despite the early hour, a few cars were parked facing the water, a seemly distance apart. Their occupants gazed out at the cove, sipped coffee, or paged through the morning newspaper, according to preference. Henry Ellis, publisher and editor-in-chief of the *Old Wethersfield Gazette*, our weekly newspaper, stood outside his car pointing his digital camera at the birds warming themselves in the early morning sun. Clara Seymour's old Dodge was tucked into its usual spot under a low-hanging tree limb down by the water's edge. Clara was the high school principal's wife. It was an open secret that she sneaked down to the cove mornings to enjoy a cigarette with her coffee, a practice of which her husband did not approve. I lifted a hand to Ephraim Marsh, the owner of Marsh Pharmacy, which had occupied the space across the street from the diner for at least three generations now, but in accordance with local etiquette, we refrained from approaching his Ford, thus intruding on what would probably be the most peaceful few moments of his day. On our way down to the water's edge, Abby Stoddard passed us in her old van en route back to the diner, her brief respite over. The new ordinance would be particularly hard on Abby, whose smoking customers had been accommodated on the brick patio behind her establishment but would soon be deprived of that privilege.

A few scruffy seagulls argued over the remains of a bran muffin, while the ducks and pigeons feigned indifference. Suddenly, a rapidly approaching flock of Canada geese honked us to attention. Emma and I exchanged broad grins and turned to watch the show. At this time of year, flocks came and went regularly, flying at night and settling onto any friendly body of water to rest and feed by day. I never tired of watching the landing ritual.

As the volume of the honking increased, the leader appeared over the tree line to our north. The rest of the flock trailed behind in an ever-widening vee-formation. Hundreds of the sleek birds soon darkened the sky above us, honking excitedly at the sight of a potential resting place. Instead of landing immediately, the leader decided to make a scouting pass. He made one complete circle of the cove, and then led his troops back over the tree line. Their sounds ebbed, and we held our breath. Had we passed muster? Did the cove meet their stringent criteria for safe harbor, or had some goosey eye spotted a suspicious glint of metal in the marsh grass that might be a hunter's rifle or some other peril, real or imaginary?

We waited five seconds, ten. Then whooping joyously, a consensus reached, the geese burst back over the trees and swooped down to the water in a graceful half-circle. The leader splashed down in the center of the cove, leaving room for his cohorts to follow suit and create a feathery blanket atop the water. They landed feet-first to slow their forward momentum, so utterly in unison that the maneuver seemed genetically choreographed. Within half a minute, they were all at rest, gabbling to each other companionably as they bobbed on the surface. Time for food and rest, and if the weather was good tonight, they would depart on another leg of their journey to more hospitable winter quarters in the Carolinas.

It was magical. Emma and I smiled happily at each other. We turned back toward the street, setting a more leisurely pace. "Grace will be an enormous help, I know," I said, picking up our conversation where we had left off, "but she can only clean around the stuff. She can't prevent it from accumulating." Grace Sajak was my twice-a-month cleaning person and a godsend to every one of her clients.

As soon as we pushed through the doors of the diner, the mingled aromas of hot coffee and cinnamon something-or-other washed over us, and we hurried to the counter to place our order. To our surprise, but not displeasure, Prudy was nowhere to be seen. Instead, we were greeted by Deenie Hewitt, the perpetually worried-looking college student who filled all the take-out orders during the morning shift before rushing off to afternoon classes.

"Hey, Emma, Miz Lawrence. Having the usual, or is this an off-your-diet day? We have some nice, fresh sticky buns."

Emma and I exchanged done-for looks. Abby's sticky buns were truly awesome. At the same moment, we said, "We'll split one," and as always, Deenie pretended to be surprised.

"Coming right up then," she said and busied herself removing one of the larger of the fragrant pastries from the doughnut tower on the counter. Deftly, she cut it in half, wrapped it up, and deposited it atop two coffees in a paper bag.

"Where's your sidekick?" Emma asked Deenie, while I dug in my jeans pocket for exact change.

Deenie shrugged, her attention already shifting to the customer in line behind us. "No clue," she said, nodding in the direction of Abby Stoddard, uncharacteristically taking an order at a booth in the rear. Normally, Abby spent her time tending to business in her cluttered office behind the kitchen. "Just didn't turn up this morning. Didn't even have the decency to call and make excuses. Miz Stoddard's fit to be tied. You have a nice day now."

We got out of her way and pushed back through the diner doors to the street. By unspoken mutual consent, we immediately rummaged in the bag for the still-warm sticky bun. We each bit deeply and groaned in ecstasy, rolling our eyes at each other as we strolled back toward the Law Barn. Three big bites and we were licking icing off our fingers as we approached the Blades Salon. We paused at the three lady scarecrows, circling around front to admire the exhibit more closely.

"This is amazing," I said, lapping shamelessly at a final drip between my thumb and forefinger. "I know they're scarecrows, but the wigs are such a great touch. Putting them in curlers and getting them to sit right on those straw noggins underneath the dryers must have taken forever." I frowned as I noticed that some disgruntled smoker, no doubt protesting the new ban, had stubbed out a filter tip in one of the saucers. "And look at the hands on the one on the left! The skin is so realistic looking against her blue dress…" I trailed off uncertainly, my stomach tightening.

I looked at Emma, who had remained motionless during my commentary, clutching the bagged coffees to her chest. She was frozen, staring at the scarecrows while the color drained from her face. "Momma?"

Not a good sign, I thought. *She only calls me Momma when she's sick. Or scared.* The little hairs on the back of my neck prickled atavistically as I approached the exhibit on stiff, unwilling legs. From across the street, the three characters in the little tableau had looked like elderly sisters, but up close, the differences jumped out. *Which of these things is not like the others?* I thought idiotically, remembering the old *Sesame Street* jingle. The lady seated on the left was the obvious answer. Although dressed in similar clothing and sporting tufts of straw at her cuffs and hemline, the hands balancing her teacup in her lap were distinctly human, unlike the knotted straw ones of her companions. The skin, though bluish in tint, looked absolutely real as did the nails, which were both dirty and broken. While it was as gray as the others, her hair was clumped hastily around a few mismatched rollers in contrast to her neatly-set seatmate. Perhaps most alarmingly, her head drooped forward to rest against the front of the dryer, hiding most of her face.

Very deliberately, Emma placed her bag on the sidewalk and came to stand next to me. I didn't want to, but I put a bracing hand against the woman's right shoulder as Emma tipped the dryer hood up and back. The full weight of the upper body sagged against me, and Emma pushed on the left shoulder to help me sit blue-dress lady upright. Wearing her habitual dour expression and a slash of duct tape over her mouth, Prudence Crane sat before us, no longer among the missing, and very dead.

"Guess we'd better let Abby know that Prudy won't be coming in today," Emma commented matter-of-factly. She dug her cell phone out of her pocket and looked at it blankly. Then she sat down hard on the curb.

Two

After taking a few deep breaths apiece, Emma and I realized that our gruesome discovery had gone unnoticed by the few pedestrians on the street. A block away, on the other side of the street, a cluster of small boys labored on their entry in the scarecrow competition, which, judging from the outdated uniform, spectacles and odd hat, seemed to be a scout leader circa 1950. Other than Miriam Drinkwater, who was letting herself into the Keeney Memorial a block farther down for her morning shift as volunteer tour guide, the only citizens to be seen at this hour were scurrying from their parked cars into the diner and back. Rather than risk pandemonium by going back inside and calling for help, we used Emma's cell phone to place a 911 call to the Wethersfield Police Department. Even though we made it clear that poor Prudy was beyond medical help, we braced ourselves for the inevitable rush of emergency vehicles that would arrive in conjunction with the official investigation that had been set into motion with our call.

I also knew that the dozens of private citizens who monitored police calls via scanners in their homes would ensure a crowd of gawkers on the scene very soon, so time was of the essence if the crime scene were to be preserved. And finally, the next person who came out of the diner would be certain to get the bare facts, then hustle back inside, bristling with self-importance, to take center stage as The First Person to Know About the Murder. The only question was, who would it be?

The answer wasn't long in coming. No sooner did our ears pick up the wail of approaching sirens than Mavis Griswold, the Methodist minister's wife, appeared from the direction of the diner. She came up behind us where we stood by the curb and paused as it became evident that the emergency vehicles were converging at the place where we stood at the entrance to Blades Salon.

"Are you all right?" she hastened to inquire, as befitted a clergyman's missus. "Is anyone hurt?"

Her long-lashed, wide-set brown eyes and pleasant expression always reminded me, most irreverently, of Elsie the Cow. Under the present somber circumstances, I admonished myself to get a grip and assured her that Emma and I were just fine. Then as gently as possible, I pointed out that Prudy Crane seemed to have gone to meet her maker, cause or causes unknown. That's when Mavis surprised me. Instead of having an attack of the vapors, she turned slowly to confront Prudy where she sat, silver duct tape covering her mouth. And then she smiled.

At the time, I didn't have an opportunity to ponder her odd reaction. A police cruiser screeched down Old Main Street from our left, followed closely by the emergency rescue van and two unmarked sedans with blue emergency lights on their dashboards. Next to arrive was the volunteer ambulance, driven at breakneck speed by Tom Clancy. Tom taught high school mathematics and lived for these occasions, which tended to elevate his standing among his students. Customers poured out of the diner to see what all the commotion was about, and arriving employees of the business establishments that lined the street soon joined the growing throng.

I was pleased to see Rick Fletcher, a young cop who had graduated from high school with Joey and one year ahead of Emma, emerge from the cruiser with his partner, who quickly began the job of backing off the crowd. Lieutenant John Harkness, the extraordinarily good-looking but perpetually dour commander of the detective division, stepped out of one of the unmarked cars. "Lieutenant Hardnose," as he was known among the locals, quickly took charge of the crime scene. Rick grabbed a reel of yellow crime scene tape and began securing the area from civilian interference. Harkness supervised the preliminary crime scene investigation. He consulted briefly with the State police team that had apparently been summoned to handle the forensics, then spoke with the investigator from the medical examiner's office, whose job it was to deal with Prudy's, ugh, body.

Once the bystanders were corralled at a safe distance, Rick's partner produced a digital camera from their cruiser and carefully photographed the assembled crowd, while Rick himself walked over to where Emma and I still sat on the curb.

"Hey, Miz Lawrence, Emma," he said politely. After checking out our ashen faces, he wisely refrained from asking us to stand up, opting instead to plunk down companionably next to Emma. "So how's your day going so far?" he asked her, straight-faced, and got the desired effect. Emma broke up, which got me giggling, and the tension was broken. A few shocked onlookers were apparently persuaded by the others that we must be having hysterics, and who could blame us, poor things, having found the body and all?

It didn't take long for Rick to get the facts from us, as there wasn't much to tell. His partner had replaced the still camera with a video cam with which he expertly panned the crime scene and the faces in the crowd. After listening to our story attentively, Rick nodded briefly and rose to his feet. "We're going to have to take you down to the station to formalize your statements," he said, offering me a discreet hand as I struggled to rise. Emma had already unfolded herself and dusted off the seat of her jeans. "It shouldn't take more than a couple of hours, but it needs to be done as fast as possible." Nodding pleasantly at the gawkers on the sidewalk, Rick lifted the yellow crime scene tape for us to duck under, then shepherded us through the crowd to where a plainclothes detective waited by one of the unmarked vehicles. "Here's your ride," he smiled and introduced us to Detective Harold Bernstein.

Looking around self-consciously, we clambered into the rear seat of the sedan and were whisked the mile or so to the Wethersfield PD's new headquarters on the Silas Deane Highway. I was relieved to note that the blue emergency light was no longer in use.

On the second floor of the pleasant, brick building, we were escorted to an interview room, where Emma was ushered in first. Police procedure dictated that we give our statements separately.

"I thought it was supposed to be age before beauty," Emma sassed me, her poise now restored. She walked into the room and looked around with interest. "What, no stenographer?"

"Sorry," said Detective Bernstein. "Literate witnesses are asked to write out their statements in longhand. You could dictate to me while I enter your statement into my laptop," he grinned apologetically, "but frankly, you're better off with the pencil and paper. Our clerical assistant will type it up before you sign it."

"So much for high-tech police techniques." She rolled her eyes. "Are you okay, 'Cita?"

"I'm perfectly happy to sit here in peace for a little while, so you just go scribble your little heart out, dearie," I assured her and sank gratefully into a visitor's chair in the sunny cubicle outside the door, where I was issued a lined pad and pencil of my own.

Nearly two hours later, our signed statements were secured, and Detective Bernstein delivered us back to the Law Barn, where we sank gratefully into the familiar territory of our work day.

Compared to the hubbub going on a few blocks away, the Monday morning chaos of the Law Barn was relatively soothing. At least here the activity had to do with the business of living, as opposed to what was taking place in front of Blades. At least, the ladies would have no shortage of gossip today, I thought, but I was afraid that Emma and I would feature prominently in the clucking. The thing was, this wasn't the first time I had discovered a body. Just about a year previously, I had been involved in a murder investigation at the law firm where Margo, Strutter and I worked. At this rate, it wouldn't be long before I became a local pariah like that lady sleuth on *Murder, She Wrote*. Everywhere she went, murder was sure to follow. I had never been able to understand why anybody invited her anywhere after the first year.

After answering the inevitable questions from Jenny, who sensibly dealt with the situation by bringing us mugs of generously sugared coffee to make up for our abandoned diner brew, Emma and I separated in the lobby. She climbed the stairs to her nook in the loft, and I climbed the few stairs down to MACK's quarters at the rear of the first floor. With Jenny screening calls from the merely curious, all was serene for half an hour as I scrambled to attend to my accumulated voice and email messages. I was prioritizing the latter when Margo sailed in from a morning showing, filled with sly glee. Rhett Butler padded beside her.

"Why, Kate, you little dickens! I know Prudy Crane kept you waitin' for your coffee a time or two, but murder? Remind me never to get on your list." She dropped her Gucci briefcase on the coffee table and draped herself elegantly on our small sofa, smoothing a stray blonde lock back into her chignon. It might not have been a trendy hairdo, but it suited Margo perfectly. Rhett sprawled at her feet and gazed at her shapely ankles with doggy adoration. "Tell me everything, Sugar."

Between phone calls—both hers and mine—I brought her up to speed on the morning's events. "Poor little Emma," was her parting comment as we walked back through the lobby together an hour later, she to another showing and I to the restroom. Rhett had been consigned to his comfortable pen in the back yard, where he could belly down in the grass and keep a watchful eye on the neighborhood cats, squirrels and chipmunks for the remainder of the morning. "This must have been Emma's first up close and personal experience with a corpse. She okay?"

"Poor little Emma is just fine," I said dryly, glancing up the stairs to the loft, from which gales of laughter emanated. "After the initial shock, she reverted to norm, thanks to that nice young police officer, Rick Fletcher. He had the good sense not to coddle her, even got her laughing."

"Hmmm, Fletcher… Fletcher. I don't believe I know the name." As fond as Margo was of attractive men in general, she was even more devoted to men in uniform and was, um, personally acquainted with a number of our local law enforcers.

"Hands off, Margo. He's my son's age, for crying out loud."

"And your point is…?" She grinned lasciviously and swayed out the door, waggling polished fingertips at Millie Haines, who was apparently just arriving for the day.

I hurried into the coatroom that occupied a niche to the right of the big barn door and approached the rear wall. Anyone unfamiliar with the Law Barn would have thought me daft, but we regulars were familiar with this architectural peculiarity. The barn itself had been built in the 1800s, and then restored in the 1950s for the enjoyment of an eccentric and extremely wealthy engineer who fancied himself an artist. Since no gallery in the Northeast seemed interested in showing his watercolors, a collection of amateurish renderings of local vistas, he created his own gallery and spared no expense restructuring and decorating the place. Several times a year, he would invite one hundred or so of his closest friends to a showing of his latest works, events that were well attended more because of the lavish spreads of food and liquor than the art hanging on the walls.

What his guests didn't know was that their host's primary entertainment during these events was concealing himself in the very room to which I was now headed. The guest bathroom was located on the other side of the lobby under the stairs and was clearly marked. This was the facility used by Law Barn clients and most of the staff. The door to the other bathroom, which only a few of us frequented, was nearly invisible in the elaborate wall paneling of the coatroom and was further obscured by the coat rack that stood in front of it. There was no exterior doorknob. To get the door to pop open, which it did silently, you had to scoot around the left end of the rack and press the paneling in exactly the right place. I did that now.

The room that was revealed was an elegantly equipped restroom, outfitted with a mahogany vanity and old-fashioned water closet with a pull chain. The exterior wall featured a floor-to-ceiling bookcase, well stocked with classic fiction, as well as pulp fiction of the '50s. A small but extraordinarily beautiful Oriental carpet covered the floor, and an overstuffed chair sat cozily in the corner along with a small end table and a lamp with a tasseled shade. When Emma introduced me and my partners to this plush hideaway, we fell in love with it immediately and vowed to keep it a delicious secret among the four of us—and Grace, of course, who kept it spotless along with the rest of the Law Barn and saw that it was stocked with fresh soap and towels. Dubbed the Reading Room, it became a welcome retreat to which we could repair to make private cell phone calls, coddle headaches and cramps, or just close our eyes for a few minutes on particularly hectic days.

It was some months after we had moved in that we discovered the reason for the secret room's existence. According to a relative of the now-deceased artist-*cum*-engineer, whose rather dreadful self-portrait hung behind Jenny's desk in the lobby, it had been especially constructed by Mr. Watercolors to indulge his favorite pastime of hide and seek. In the middle of one of his parties, he would disappear from view, only to reappear disconcertingly next to some guests who had thought they were engaged in private conversation. Watercolors waited comfortably in his secret lair until his guests had consumed enough alcohol to be indiscreet. Then up he would pop, creeping about and eavesdropping. In this way, he was able to glean not only his visitors' real opinions of his paintings but many bits of gossip that came in handy in his business dealings.

My partners and Emma and I enjoyed the story and the room itself. It offered complete privacy and sanctuary from obnoxious clients. It was also enormous fun to have a hidey-hole into which we could vanish right under the noses of staff and visitors.

As I enjoyed the scent of the special tulip hand soap we kept on the vanity, images from the morning tumbled chaotically through my mind... the wild geese on the cove, Emma's shocked face, Mavis Griswold's pleased smile. It had been an odd reaction to the situation, to say the least. Had I imagined it? No, I had not. It had crept across Mavis' face against her will, I was sure. I debated the wisdom of mentioning it to Lt. Harkness. Drying my hands on the fresh guest towel Grace had provided, I decided to consult Emma before making up my mind one way or the other.

As always before exiting the Reading Room, I listened at the crack of the door to make sure no one was in the coat room before making my exit, then headed for the stairs up to the loft. One needn't worry about startling Emma, whose desk sat in an airy but cluttered recess at the top of the staircase, since the old wood creaked at every step. In any event, she was on the phone, which was pretty much a chronic state of being during her workday.

"Hi, Icky," I greeted the young field mouse who resided in a hamster cage on the credenza behind her desk. The old building housed its share of mice, and my tender-hearted daughter was forever rescuing one or another from the next door neighbor's cat, a bruiser named Jake, and rehabilitating it before releasing it behind the barn. Each mouse was named Icky, due to visitors' tendency to cry, "Ooooh, ick!" when they noticed the rodent *du jour*. The current patient was not only alive but feisty, rushing around bumping into the glass sides of his enclosure.

"I think this one's about ready to go," I told Emma when she hung up the phone. "He's starting to throw himself at the glass." A wildlife biologist at the nature center had warned us that such behavior indicated release was warranted.

Emma nodded. "I know. I'll take him out back on my way to lunch. Jake will probably eat him for dinner, but at least I gave the kid a second chance." She shrugged philosophically. "What's up?"

I told her about Mavis Griswold's inexplicable reaction to the news of Prudy's death and asked her opinion. "I'm inclined to mention it to the lieutenant, but I want to be sure I'm not just scandal-mongering. What do you think? Am I overreacting here?"

"Hard to say," Emma replied thoughtfully. "Obviously, there's a story there somewhere, but who knows what it might be? Maybe grinning is just a nervous reaction for Mavis, although one would hope not, her being a minister's wife and all. Have you considered just asking her about it straight out?"

I hadn't, but I did now. "Okay. I guess I could do that. It might be a little embarrassing for both of us, but it beats pointing suspicion at her if there's no reason to do so." I glanced around. Jimmy's door was closed, as usual, and nobody else was in sight. "Where is everybody?"

"Out to lunch, of course. They got all the gory details they could out of me, so they went in search of fresh dirt and left me to hold the fort." The phone rang again, and she grimaced. "Emma here," she said into the receiver, then mouthed "See you later" at me. I retraced my steps to the first floor.

The rest of the day was filled with the usual end-of-month crises. Anyone involved with the business of transferring real estate knows that more closings are scheduled during the last week of the month than during the previous three weeks combined, and our personal lives get put on hold for the duration. With the ability to transfer documents electronically, and the repeal of the Blue Laws that used to protect our Sundays, weekends were no longer an exception. On the first of each month, our lives returned to normal, but until then, refrigerators remained empty, laundry went undone, and errands accumulated while we tended nonstop to business.

Sharing office space with Emma and her boss was working well. Both businesses benefited from mutual referrals, and Emma had the patience I lacked with the nervous first-time property buyers who were my particular peeve. Bristling with self-importance and their cutting-edge knowledge of real estate practices, usually obtained from a 22-year-old nephew or a library book written in 1987, they entered into the transaction determined that nobody was going to pull the wool over their eyes but convinced that everybody was trying to do just that. My reassurances that the people with whom we worked were consummate professionals, and really nice folks besides, tended to fall on deaf ears, and I quickly lost patience with those clients' bad attitudes. Emma, however, simply ignored their bullying and set them straight, quietly but firmly, and few could look into her honest brown eyes and doubt her word.

At nearly six o'clock, I turned off my computer and rubbed my eyes, grainy from staring at a lighted screen all afternoon. I walked out through the lobby, which was windowless and thus almost dark, and stuck my head up the stairwell to the loft. As I expected, Emma's lights were still on, and I could hear her soothing yet another jittery client on the phone. "Goodnight, Sweetie, don't stay too much later," I called and let myself out the big barn door, turning my key in the outside lock to keep the bogeyman away from my girl.

When I arrived at my condominium, I was surprised to see lights gleaming through the kitchen windows and two cars parked end to end on one side of the driveway—Joey's Honda and Manny's Passat. *Uh oh.* It had completely slipped my mind that Joey was coming for dinner tonight, and Manny's visit was unscheduled. Guiltily, I pressed the automatic door opener on my visor and waited for the garage door to rise. Manny and Joey were uncomfortable in each other's presence. It was partly age and ethnicity, I knew. After all, how much could a middle-aged Latino raised in South America and a twenty-something Caucasian raised in New England have in common? But more than that, it was temperament. Manny was reserved and gentlemanly, Joey was open and flamboyant. They just didn't get each other. For my sake, they made polite conversation when trapped in the same room, but their mutual confusion was always evident.

I eased open the car door and tiptoed to the top of the short staircase that led from the garage to the kitchen, where I pressed my ear to the door. I heard nothing but the hiss of something sautéing on the stove and the clink of a pet tag on the edge of Jasmine's, or more likely Simon's, kitty chow bowl. My beloved old cat Oliver had died the previous spring. While I was still grieving, my next door neighbor, an elderly woman named Mary Feeney, appeared one evening cuddling a furry mite to her chest. She had found the kitten dodging cars in the supermarket parking lot and brought him to me for temporary shelter. Within two days, I couldn't give him up. The mite, named Simon, had made it a point never to miss another meal and currently tipped the scales at seventeen pounds.

I tiptoed back down to the car, chunked its door shut, and then clattered back up the stairs. "I'm home!" I announced cheerfully as I burst through the door. The kitchen was empty but for Jasmine, licking her whiskers after her dinner, but an enticing aroma of cooking wafted from a covered pan on the stovetop. Raucous laughter came from the family room. "What's so funny?" I asked, coming into the room and dropping my raincoat over Joey's blond head where he lay on the sofa with Simon sandbagging his broad chest. Manny, in office attire and groomed to perfection, as always, rose to give me a quick kiss, and I patted his backside appreciatively before Joey struggled out from under my coat. Both wore the guilty expressions of "Men Caught in the Act..." of what, I didn't know. *An off-color joke? Woman-bashing?* I wrote it off to a little male bonding and didn't pursue it.

An hour later, we finished up the tasty entree concocted by Manny out of rice and some leftover chicken and fresh tomatoes he'd found in the refrigerator, and I finished telling them the surprising events of the day. Both greeted my news in character.

"I am sorry you had such a distressing day, *Cara*," said Armando, taking my hand, "but at least this time, you are not in any danger." This last part referred to the murder that had occurred a year previously, which Margo, Strutter and I had helped to solve.

"Yeah, this getting involved in murder investigations is getting to be a habit with you, Ma. It's a little kinky, but if you and the girls get tired of real estate, you can always get your P.I. licenses," Joey chuckled.

I glared. "I am not involved in a murder investigation. I merely found the body. And 'the girls' are the same age as your mother, roughly speaking, so kindly show a little respect."

Joey dumped Jas and Simon from his lap, where they had been jockeying for position, then stacked up our plates and headed for the kitchen to load the dishwasher. "Whatever you say, you old bat," he agreed cheerfully.

"How did I manage to raise two completely disrespectful offspring?" I called after him.

"What goes around comes around," he yelled back, and I let him have the last word. He probably had a point. After crashing plates and cutlery into the dishwasher, he rejoined us to make his farewells. "So long, Ma," he said, enveloping me in his usual bear hug, and I wondered for the hundredth time how a colicky, six-pound infant had morphed into this strapping young man who routinely wrestled 70-foot tractor trailer rigs over the highways and byways.

"Be a good boy," I delivered as my part of our silly farewell ritual, a gesture to the old days. It was my personal talisman to keep him safe during the long night of driving ahead of him.

Releasing me, Joey turned to Manny and leaned forward as if to give him a smooch. Instinctively, Manny recoiled in macho horror, and Joey cracked up. "Gotcha, Man!" he triumphed as Manny rolled his eyes. Then he rumpled the cats' fur and was gone, leaving the house oddly quiet after the kitchen door banged shut behind him.

"So," said Manny.

"So."

"How are you doing with all of this?"

"Better now," I said, enjoying his scent of soap and expensive cologne as I nestled against his cashmere covered chest.

"And Emma? How is she doing?"

I considered. Being the center of a drama during the workday was one thing. How was she faring alone in her apartment after this difficult day? I reached for the wireless and punched in her number, but all I got was her recorded message. Between boyfriends at the moment, she was either out with one or another of her many girlfriends or sound asleep with the ringer off. Either way, I knew intellectually she was fine, but the mom part of me fretted a bit. "Guess she's having an early night," I concluded, replacing the phone in its charger.

"Probably a good idea," Manny smiled. I smiled back, and without further discussion, we headed for my bedroom. The phone rang, and I groaned.

"Yes," I answered distractedly, expecting to hear Emma's voice. Instead, Abby Stoddard spoke into my ear.

"Sorry to bother you, Kate," she apologized, "but frankly, I just didn't know where else to turn, and you having experience with this sort of thing… well, I thought you might be willing to help me sort something out." Abby sounded uncharacteristically flustered, as well she might, after the day she'd had.

Inwardly, I cringed. As intriguing as the events of last year had been, they had left me with the fervent hope that I would never again be forced to delve into other people's personal lives. I preferred to live in blissful ignorance. Still, Abby had been very helpful to us over the past year, filling us in on the vicissitudes of running a business in a small town, and a friend was a friend. "You bet, Abby. What can I do?"

There was a short silence. "I'm not sure what anybody can do," she said finally, "but I need somebody else to know what's been happening before it's too late. Meet me at the diner when you can tomorrow, will you?"

"Well, sure, but what do you mean, 'before it's too late'?" I asked, not really wanting to know.

"Before someone else is murdered," she said flatly and broke the connection.

Three

Abby Stoddard came from a long line of Stoddards, most of whom lay at rest in the Reverend Dr. Henry Griswold's churchyard diagonally across the street from the *Village Diner*. You couldn't travel the length of Wethersfield without running across a road, building or other memorial to one or another of her ancestors. For as long as anyone could remember, she had kept company with Frank Wainwright, the previous owner of the diner and about 10 years her senior, but the two had never married. "Just not the marrying kind, neither one of us," Abby explained without apology, but they were as much a couple as the longest-married pair in town. For the most part, their devotion was unquestioned, but until Frank's death a few years previously, they had endured the scorn of a few self-righteous prigs, particularly when Abby took Frank into her home to care for him during his final illness, "and them not even married in the sight of God!" But even the most vocal critics fell silent when at last the cancer claimed poor Frank, and he left the diner to Abby in his will—lock, stock and trash barrels.

I thought about how difficult those next few years must

have been for Abby as I walked down the street to the diner the next afternoon. Running a restaurant, even one as well established as this one, was a tricky business. Keeping ahead of expenses was a challenge for an experienced owner, let alone someone with no experience whatsoever. Still, Abby had dug in and somehow managed to keep the place afloat, keeping a roof over her head and that of her aged mother in the bargain.

The crime scene tape in front of the antiques shop and Blades had been removed, and the scarecrows and their props had been hauled off by the police for forensic examination. Fortunately—or unfortunately, depending upon your point of view—our little murder hadn't deterred the tourists who flocked to see this year's crop of scarecrows. If anything, the crowds were bigger and earlier than most years, the locals assured me. Although most of the sightseers parked down at the cove and walked up the hill, we had noticed the increase in traffic at our end of the street, too. Usually, parking was at a premium only on weekends, but now it was becoming difficult for our clients to find a place to park during the week.

I had deliberately waited until mid-afternoon when there would be a lull between the lunch and dinner rushes. As if she were expecting me, Abby sat at the counter with a cup of coffee as I pushed through the swinging door from the sidewalk. Trim and petite, Abby might have passed for forty were it not for the graying hair that she had decided to ignore and the worry lines that had etched themselves into her otherwise youthful forehead. The place was empty except for Mort Delahanty, the seedy-looking, middle-aged fellow who swept under the tables, emptied the trash, cleaned the restrooms, and performed other menial chores around the diner. As far as anyone knew, Mort didn't speak. He certainly never had to me. He scowled wordlessly at me now and went back to refilling salt shakers.

I was surprised to see a cigarette smoldering between Abby's fingers and raised my eyebrows. "I know. You'd think watching Frank die of lung cancer would have been enough to put me off the things, but..." her voice trailed off, and she shrugged. "Frank needed to smoke. I hated it. So we accommodated each other. He didn't smoke around me, and I never complained when he stepped outside for a cigarette. The hard thing now is knowing that if I'd been a little less accommodating, Frank might still be alive."

"So you punish yourself by smoking?"

Abby looked at me a moment but didn't reply. "Thanks for coming by, Kate. Let's go back to my office." She stubbed out the cigarette in her saucer and led the way through the kitchen to the cramped quarters that served as her office. A wooden desk overflowed with order forms, invoices, timesheets, and a huge, old-fashioned ledger. A computer workstation lurked in the corner, covered with dust. It looked as if it had never been turned on. Cartons of office supplies, samples, and unfiled correspondence were shoved against the wall. Abby scraped a pile of newspapers and catalogs off the wooden guest chair in front of her desk and motioned me into it. Instead of sitting herself, she folded her arms across her chest and started to pace back and forth behind the desk.

"I hope you didn't just have lunch, because what I have to tell you is pretty gruesome. Do you remember when you found Prudy, her mouth was covered with duct tape?"

I nodded, dreading what I might hear next. With good reason, it turned out.

"Everyone knows by now that Prudy was poisoned."

"I didn't. What kind of poison?"

"The medical examiner says chlordane. It's a very deadly chemical commonly found in industrial strength cleaners. You know, the kind of cleaner you'd use in a restaurant." She stopped pacing and looked at me. "And that's not all."

I tried mightily to keep my expression neutral. "Okay. What else?"

Abby's mouth twisted in disgust. "When they took the tape off, they discovered that Prudy's tongue had been cut out. Hacked right off with a kitchen knife. Sorry!" she added, as my stomach roiled in protest, and I felt suddenly faint. I lowered my head into one hand and held up the other to ward off further horrific revelations, momentarily unable to speak. Abby walked over and patted me on the back briefly, but there was no stemming the flow of words. She plowed on, determined to get it all out.

"That wasn't what killed her, of course. It was the poison. As a matter of fact, her tongue was cut out after she was dead. Otherwise, her mouth would have been filled with blood when they took the tape off."

That did it. I fell forward and stuck my head all the way down between my knees as the room spun around me. Taking serious note of my plight at last, Abby crouched next to me, rubbing my back and making soothing noises. "I know, it's a shock. You'll feel better in a minute. Do you want some water?"

I nodded. I didn't want any water, but getting some would get her out of the room for a couple of minutes and give me a chance to regroup. She opened the door and went out, and I breathed shallowly through my mouth so I wouldn't hyperventilate. By the time Abby returned with a glass of ice water, I had recovered sufficiently to sit upright again. I accepted the water gratefully.

"Sorry, Abby. I've always been a little squeamish. You should have seen me at the emergency room when Joey accidentally stabbed himself in the leg with a pair of my sewing scissors about twenty years ago. I'm better now."

Abby got to her feet. "The thing is, Kate, it was my knife. It came right out of the diner's kitchen, and it had my fingerprints all over it." She sagged suddenly into her desk chair and put her forehead into her hands. "I'm the number one suspect. They think I did it. They haven't actually arrested me, but that could happen any time now."

As shocked as I had been by Abby's words, I was even more shocked at the idea of her being anyone's murderer. Abby Stoddard had nursed Frank through his final illness. She had taken her aged mother into her home. And it was Abby who had given Prudy Crane a job when nobody else in town would. Outrage helped me find my tongue.

"That's ridiculous. I don't know you all that well, but even I know you're incapable of killing anyone. For God's sake, Deenie told me that you use Have-A-Heart mousetraps in your pantry. Who in the world would try to pin this on you?"

Abby lifted her head and stared into space over my shoulder. "The police, that's who. It was my knife, Kate. It had my prints on it."

"That's circumstantial. Of course the knife had your prints on it. You probably used it every day. I take it you have no alibi for the time of death? When was that, anyway?"

"As far as the medical examiner could determine, the chlordane killed her sometime around midnight Sunday. The tongue was cut off after that. Then the body was propped up outside Blades sometime in the wee hours, judging by how much blood pooled in the lower part of it."

My head swam again, and I struggled to stay focused. "What about an alibi?"

"I was doing paperwork right here until about ten o'clock. Prudy had left at six. I assume she went back to her apartment in the old Wheeler house. I was just glad she was gone. When I locked up, I drove around for a while to clear my head, then went home and got into bed. Mom was already asleep, so I didn't wake her up just to say goodnight. I was exhausted and fell asleep almost immediately. No witnesses," she joked feebly.

"Even so, that's all perfectly normal stuff for you. You always do the bookkeeping on Sunday night. Even I know that, because once when Margo and I were working late on a Sunday, we tried to get a sandwich, but even though the lights were on, the door was locked. You must have been here in the back room. A passer-by told us it was your custom to catch up on paperwork on Sunday nights."

"Huh! Everybody knows everything in a small town."

"I still don't see how the police have enough to arrest you. After all, you were the one that kept Prudy employed, even though she was a lousy waitress. There must be something else the police know that we don't."

"I know what it is." She leaned back in her chair and met my eyes. "Prudy was blackmailing me, and the police found out about it. They looked into my books, and there were discrepancies…" her voice trailed off.

Well, that would explain why you kept her on the payroll, I thought, but I kept my mouth shut and waited.

Pure hatred blazed from Abby's eyes. "Prudence Crane was a vicious, scheming, horror of a woman, but the plain fact is, without her on my side, I would have lost the diner… and I need this business."

"Because of your mother?" I prompted

Abby nodded. "When Frank was alive, he helped out a lot. When he became so ill, I took on Prudy because I needed the help, but the only person that harpy ever helped was herself." She laughed without humor. "One day, I had to leave her in charge for the dinner rush. Frank had been rushed to the hospital again, and he needed me with him. It was very late when I got back to the diner. It had been closed for hours." She paused as if weighing the wisdom of confiding in me further. Then she made her decision.

"Prudy greeted me at the door that night. She had the register tapes and the order slips from the previous week spread out on the counter. They didn't match. It hadn't taken her long to figure out that a lot of the cash business had never gone through the register." Abruptly, she stood and resumed her restless pacing. Or maybe she simply didn't want to look at me as she continued.

"My expenses were through the roof. There was the medicine and all of the other things Mom needed. Extra help in the house while I was with Frank so much. And of course, he wasn't able to help me financially any longer. So I started pocketing most of the cash from the orders I took myself, not reporting it to the government. I believe they call it income tax fraud," she said. Her expression was bleak. "I didn't know what else to do. I thought it would just be for a few weeks, a couple of months, maybe. And then it went on and on, and I forgot to throw out the order slips for the cash I'd skimmed, and, well…" She turned to face me.

"There's no way to excuse it. I just did it, that's all. And Prudy found out about it and announced that she would keep my little secret if I'd keep hers. I asked her what she meant, but she just smiled to herself and didn't say anything." Abby dropped back into her chair and rubbed her temples.

I felt myself staring in disbelief and consciously rearranged my features into what I hoped was a compassionate expression. *Poor Abby.* What a spot to be in, held over a barrel by a blackmailer. "Did you ever find out what Prudy meant, what her secret was?"

"Oh, yes," Abby assured me. "For a few days after that, I was too rattled to pay much attention to what was going around me. Mostly, I just tried to keep out of Prudy's way. But I guess my brain was working in spite of myself, and it started keeping track of her activities pretty closely. It took a while, but I finally noticed that we had several regular customers every weeknight who always sat at Prudy's station. That in itself was hard to explain, her being such a bad waitress and all. But what really caught my attention was that most of them only ordered coffee."

"What's so strange about that? Maybe they knew that was about all she could handle and played it safe."

"It wasn't the coffee. It was the fact that they almost never drank it. And then there was the way they paid for it—with big bills, always with big bills. One night, I saw Prudy slide a fifty-dollar bill into the pocket of that ratty old sweater she always wore around here. It never made it into the cash register. Being experienced at that sort of thing myself by that time, I got her alone and confronted her. She just grinned at me with those bad teeth of hers. 'We all have our little secrets now, don't we, Miz Stoddard?' she said.

"After that, she didn't bother to hide it from me. She and I were the only ones behind the counter most nights. And two or three nights a week, her victims paid her off in cash. They just put the cash under their checks and walked out. A lot of our regulars leave cash on the counter, so I never thought anything of it until I saw her pocket that fifty."

"Understandable," I said, although my head was reeling. I thought carefully before asking my next question. "Who was she blackmailing besides you, Abby, and why?"

"I don't know why, but I know who, or at least I know who some of her victims were. The thing is, I don't want to tell the police unless I absolutely have to. You know how small towns are, you just gave me an example.

Everybody knows everybody else's business and gossips like crazy about it. My telling the police that Prudy was blackmailing these folks would be just the same as accusing each and every one of them of murder." She dropped her hands from her temples and leaned forward. "For myself, it doesn't matter so much. Half the people in this town probably wonder why it took me so long to do that woman in and figure I'll plead temporary insanity or something. But the others… even if they're never charged with murder, the fact that they had secrets dark enough that they submitted to blackmail will ruin them."

I nodded in agreement, knowing what she said was true. These fifth- and sixth-generation New Englanders wouldn't do business with anyone who had submitted to blackmail. *Where's there's smoke, there's fire, and all that.* "Why are you telling me all this, Abby? What do you want me to do?"

Then Abby did something I never would have expected. She reached over the desk and covered my hand with her own. "I didn't kill Prudy, Kate, but someone did. The other people she was blackmailing are the most likely candidates I can think of, but right now, I'm the only one the police know about. I'm their only suspect. To clear myself without implicating anyone else, I've got to find out which of her blackmail victims really did it. I heard you investigated something like this before, so you'd know what to do." Her eyes sought mine. "Can you help me out?"

A long minute passed while all the reasons why I shouldn't become involved in this mess whirled through my head. None of them seemed terribly compelling compared to the tacit plea in Abby's eyes.

"Yes," I said. "Who were Prudy's other victims, Abby?"

Still, she hesitated.

"I promise you that I'll reveal nothing that I don't absolutely have to."

"Not even to me," she insisted. "I honestly don't want to know my customers' secrets."

I knew what she meant. Already, I dreaded the burden of knowing what I was about to learn about my neighbors. Generally speaking, I'm happier operating on a need-to-know basis when it comes to the details of other people's lives. "Not even to you," I assured her.

Abby reached into her apron pocket and watched my face closely as she handed me a folded scrap of white paper. *She's the one in big trouble here,* I thought, *but she looks as if she's feeling sorry for me.* And then I understood why.

On the paper were written three names: Ephraim Marsh, Mavis Griswold, and Emma Lawrence.

Four

I was rehashing the surprising developments of the afternoon with Margo. I had promised Abby I would discuss it with no one else, but I needed Margo's advice. For all of her libidinous, southern belle affectations, Margo Farnsworth was one of the most levelheaded people I knew. Besides, she had been through a murder investigation with me once before, when one of the partners at the law firm we both worked for turned up dead.

We were sitting at each end of the sofa in my family room, Rhett Butler lolling luxuriously between us, his head in Margo's lap. As long as he remained motionless, which he seemed happy to do, Jasmine and Simon accepted his presence warily from where they were curled up, rump to rump, in front of the fireplace, but if he lifted his head, I knew they would evanesce in the way that cats can. A piece of driftwood Manny had picked up during one of our walks on the beach at Harkness Memorial Park last summer added snap and color to the blaze, a welcome distraction from the darkness that came on fast. In another few weeks, Daylight Saving Time would end, and the dark season would be upon us in earnest.

Margo took a long, unladylike pull from the bottle of beer she held. I sipped more cautiously at an excellent Pinot Grigio. "No matter how hard I try, I cannot cast Abigail Stoddard as anyone's cold-blooded murderer, not even Prudy's," I said wearily. "I can believe she would lash out against someone who was threatening her life or her mother's, or even her dog's, if it came to that. But not premeditated murder, uh-uh."

"So we assume it's not Abby, but can you honestly picture any of the three people whose names are on that piece of paper stabbin' Prudence Crane to death and then hackin' out her tongue? Oh, sorry, Sugar," she apologized hastily as I covered my mouth with my hand and set my wineglass down hard. "It's difficult to believe that the mother of two can go all wobbly during any discussion involvin' blood."

"Margo!"

"Okay, okay. All I mean is, if it's not Abby, then who could it be? The minister's wife? That absolutely lovely man who owns the drugstore? Way too Gothic for me, hon. Or how about your own daughter as a likely suspect? What in the world is Emma doin' on that list anyway?"

"Believe me, she and I are going to have a conversation about that very soon," I assured her. "Obviously, it's a mistake of some kind. Abby thought she saw something she didn't, that's all. I hope," I muttered into my wineglass.

Margo drained her bottle of beer and belched genteelly. "Well, naturally," she said, and then got down to business in typical Margo fashion. "Now tell me, Sugar. How can I help?"

"I only wish I knew," I said, then almost immediately had an idea. "We need information that will keep Abby from being arrested, and that means redirecting the police department's attention, right?"

Margo's eyes began to glitter lasciviously. "Why, I believe I've redirected the attention of a police officer or two in my time," she smiled.

"Mmmm, I'll bet you have," I agreed, "and I need you to do it again. Do you remember my telling you about John Harkness, or Lieutenant Hardnose, as he's known around town?"

Margo nodded. "That nice young Fletcher fellow's boss, the one who's directin' the investigation."

"That's the one. Harkness has a reputation for being close-mouthed, won't talk to the press any more than absolutely necessary, that sort of thing. So the public, which in this case is us, knows very little about the progress of the investigation. Oh, we know the approximate time and cause of death, what the medical examiner had to say, the stuff that's public information, but beyond that, we're clueless. We don't know how close they are to making an arrest, or who besides Abby might be considered a suspect or even anyone else who's been questioned. We don't know what Prudy's movements were the night she was killed, or who else might have been with her. For that matter, we don't know if the police know she was blackmailing anybody besides Abby, because Abby hasn't told them yet."

"And you want to know if they already know that."

"Yep. Because if they do, then there's no percentage in

Abby keeping what she knows about these other people to herself. In fact, keeping her mouth shut could make her look like Prudy's accomplice."

"You're not makin' any sense, hon. How could Abby be accused of bein' Prudy's accomplice *and* her murderer at the same time? Oh!" she said as she suddenly understood what I meant.

"That's right. What better motive for murder than getting rid of your partner in extortion and keeping all the payoffs for yourself?"

"I do see your point." Thoughtfully, Margo stroked Rhett between his silky ears. He groaned with pleasure, causing Jasmine and Simon to open their eyes and assess the situation. The dog didn't move, and the cats downgraded from orange alert to yellow caution.

"So what do you think? Can you manage to get an interview with Harkness on some ruse or other and loosen up his tongue so we have a better idea of where to go on this thing?"

Margo held her empty beer bottle out to me, and I rose to get her another. "That extraordinarily good-lookin' Lieutenant?" She winked. "Why, it'll be like fallin' off a log, Sugar. You just leave the good commander to me."

~ * ~

I had no doubt that Margo's conversation with Lieutenant Harkness would be productive, but my own conversation with Emma didn't go exactly as I had hoped. The next day was particularly rushed, it being the last week of the month, and I practically had to drag Emma out of the *Law Barn* for a mother-daughter *tête-à-tête*. We were further delayed by Emma's detour to put out some peanuts for Fat Squirrel, another of her rehab cases. The peanuts were his reward on days when he stayed out of the Law Barn's trash cans, which he raided regularly. Emma had decided to try positive reinforcement. I had my doubts.

Eventually, we headed for a take-out lunch from The Spicy Green Bean, a little eatery down the street from the diner. The menu changed daily, depending upon such ephemera as a bumper crop of zucchini (soup and pasta), a crate of citrus shipped by an auntie in Florida (fruit salad), and the culinary whims of its owners. ("It just felt like a macaroni and cheese day!") About the only thing you could count on was that whatever was on the menu would be tasty and reasonably priced. Apparently, that was enough, because the lunch-hour business boomed, especially on a day as nice as this. The September sun warmed our shoulders as we queued up at the take-out window, and a breeze flirted with the weighted-down napkins of those lucky enough to find seats at the half-dozen round tables set out on the wide, brick sidewalk. A few were occupied by defiant smokers, determined to enjoy their dwindling opportunities to puff in public.

As we waited, I smiled nervously at my daughter and wondered how I was going to broach the subject of her alleged payoff to Prudy Crane. Emma smiled back sunnily, her eyes clear, her brow unfurrowed, the picture of innocence. Was she, I wondered as do all parents who have the sense God gave a goose, or was I being blind and stupid?

Eventually, we secured our chicken-and-basil salads and paper cartons of homemade split pea soup and carried them across the street to the Methodist churchyard, where we sat on the laprobe I kept in my car with our backs comfortably against a tree at the edge of the peaceful cemetery. Emma turned her face up to the sun and closed her eyes, enjoying the respite from the telephone. She knew better than to turn her cell phone on when she was with me, knowing how I loathed the intrusive things. I sipped my soup and wondered how to begin. I needn't have worried.

"So what's up, 'Cita?" Emma inquired without opening her eyes. "We don't 'do lunch,' so something is obviously on your mind. Let's hear it."

I couldn't help smiling at her untroubled countenance. *Right to the point, as usual.* I responded in kind. "It turns out that Prudy Crane was a blackmailer. I know it's true, because Abby Stoddard was among her victims, and she told me so herself." I paused to assess Emma's reaction to this news. She opened her eyes and looked closely at me but said nothing. I sipped again, my heart beating faster.

"That revelation, the fact that Prudy was poisoned with a cleaning solution Abby kept in her cupboard, and the further fact that Prudy's tongue was cut out with a knife from the diner's kitchen pretty much puts Abby at the top of the suspect list." Again, I waited for some comment, but Emma stayed silent. She dropped her eyes and busied herself by pushing her salad around with a plastic fork. Suddenly, I was filled with dread. "So what do you think, Em?"

For a moment, Emma continued to push cucumber chunks and cherry tomatoes around in the plastic container. Then she raised her eyes to mine. The sadness I saw in them did nothing to allay my fears. "I think Abby Stoddard probably had every reason in the world to murder that vicious gossip. I also think she didn't do it."

A wave of nausea washed over me, and I lowered my soup to the grass. My hands began to shake, and I clasped them together in my lap.

If she's about to confess to the murder of Prudence Crane, I've got to keep it together so that I can help her get through this, thought Hysteric Kate wildly. *Oh, get hold of yourself, Emma didn't kill anybody,* chimed in Rational Kate. *She saves mice from the neighborhood tomcat, for crying out loud.*

I took a deep breath and held it, waiting. Miriam Drinkwater emerged from the diner across the street and strolled back toward the Keeney Memorial for her afternoon shift. She lifted a hand to us, and I controlled my trembling long enough to return her wave.

"Wh—" I cleared my throat and tried again. "What makes you think so?"

"Because too many other people had better reasons to do it without putting so much at risk," Emma said steadily. "I've worked in this town longer than you have, remember, and I've heard more of the gossip. Abby needs to make a living for herself and her mom. She couldn't afford to jeopardize that. It was just a matter of time until somebody else took her off Prudy's hook. She just had to wait."

I spoke carefully, my eyes searching hers. "And what do you know about being on Prudy's hook?"

For the first time, Emma smiled. "I didn't do her in, if that's what you're so worried about. Oh, don't get me wrong. There were many days when I could have strangled Prudy Crane cheerfully, but Sunday wasn't one of them. She was as annoying as hell, but she didn't have anything on me." She reached across my lap and retrieved my soup cup from the grass, where it was about to tip over. "So unclench your fists, and have your lunch." She handed me the cup with a reassuring pat and picked up her salad again. "You really are being ridiculous, you know?"

Relief swept through me, followed quickly by anger. "If I'm so ridiculous, why were you seen paying Prudy off at the diner two weeks ago?" I said brutally and was gratified when she choked on the chicken she was chewing and had a coughing fit. I thumped her between her shoulder blades rather harder than necessary and handed her a tissue from my purse. She stopped coughing and blew her nose. I waited for whatever the benign explanation was for the "payoff" Abby had supposedly witnessed, but none was forthcoming.

"So you know about that, too," Emma said resignedly when she could speak again, and my emotional rollercoaster hit the downslope once again.

"Cheer up. Apparently, there's still quite a bit I don't know," I said tersely. "I don't suppose you care to enlighten me."

Emma regarded me somberly. "No can do, 'Cita. Not this time."

I stared at her. "You're kidding, right? No," I plowed on as a particularly mulish expression I recognized from Emma's adolescence swept over her features and turned her eyes stubborn, "I can see that you're not kidding. Well, listen up. This isn't high school, Emma, where the worst thing that could happen is a couple of days' suspension. This is a real-world, in-your-face murder investigation, and the stakes are a whole lot higher. No matter how extreme the provocation may have been for murdering Prudy Crane, someone is going to jail for life— or possibly heading for a lethal injection. I'd just as soon it wasn't you. I didn't ask to get involved in this situation, but Abigail Stoddard asked for my help, and I am surely going to give it to her. Doing so means I have to find out why several other people were allowing themselves to be extorted over the past few months. You're on that list. Now are you going to help me out here by explaining why?"

Carefully, Emma repacked her untouched soup and remaining salad in the paper sack provided by the restaurant and dusted imaginary crumbs from her lap. "I haven't been in high school for quite a few years now. But as much as I hated it at the time, I wish I was right back there, because from where I sit now, it looks pretty damned good." She blinked back tears that threatened to spill down her cheeks. "I know you're in a tough spot, and I'm sorry about that, truly. But I can't tell you what you want to know without putting someone else in the jackpot, and I just won't do that." She looked at me pleadingly. "Please try to understand."

As quickly as it had come, my anger disappeared, only to be replaced by the dread I had felt ever since Abby had handed me that slip of paper bearing Emma's name. "If you won't tell me, I'll have to find out some other way, Emma."

"No, you really don't have to do that."

"What are my options?"

"You could simply take my word for it that I'm not involved in Prudy Crane's murder."

I was silent for a moment. *Honest, Mom, I wasn't drinking last night. Nobody at the party had drugs. Trust me.* "I do take your word for it, but the police won't."

"How are the police going to know, if you don't tell them?"

"For God's sake, Emma, they'll know about it the same way I know about it! Abby Stoddard is days from being arrested for murder. She is hoping against hope that in order to save herself, she doesn't have to point suspicion at anyone else, which is why she's asked for my help. But if there's no other choice, she's going to have to tell the police about the other people she knows for a fact were paying Prudy off, and that includes you!"

It was Emma's turn to be silent. Then, "Well, then there's only one thing left to do," she said. To my utter astonishment, she smiled, her brown eyes mischievous.

"I can hardly wait to hear this," I said faintly. "What?"

"We have to find out who the real killer is. That way, Abby will be cleared and no one else will have to be implicated except the murderer."

I stared at her some more. "We?"

"Sure. I'll help you. It's only fair." She sprang nimbly to her feet and held out a hand. "Besides, it will be fun."

"Fun." I allowed her to haul me to my feet. I really had to stop sitting on the ground.

"Okay, interesting, then." She stooped to retrieve the remains of my lunch. "So where do we start?"

My head was starting to spin again. How had I lost

control of this situation so completely? This conversation hadn't turned out at all the way it was supposed to. I put a hand on the cemetery fence to steady myself and gazed at the church beyond it. Doing so reminded me of the other names on the list Abby had given me and Mavis Griswold's strange smile when she saw Prudy Crane's body outside the Blades Salon. What choice did I have? Emma was right. If I were to help Abby and avoid pointing suspicion at my daughter, I was going to have to discover the real murderer. I sighed.

"Mavis Griswold," I said. "That's where we start."

Five

As if we didn't have enough on our minds, the end of the month crunch was upon us, and Emma and I were sucked back into the madness as soon as we returned to the Law Barn. Margo cut off all but essential showings and pitched in on the phones and scheduling with Jenny and me while Emma and her colleagues cranked out packages for the fourteen closings that were scheduled over the next two days. As always during these periods, we were only marginally aware of what was going on in the outside world, but every so often, when the front door opened, we could hear the chanting of the protestors in front of the Keeney Memorial across the street. It was a subdued protest, but a protest nonetheless, and business owners up and down the street experienced the effects of these bad feelings in the reduced foot traffic on Old Main Street. It wasn't looking good for the weekend, either. Not only would the protestors still be at it, discouraging visitors and local customers both, but the weather forecast called for rain.

With difficulty, I managed to find two minutes to telephone the church rectory and arrange an appointment with Mrs. Griswold for the following afternoon. She was understandably bewildered by my request, since I had never set foot in the church, but I made up a story about wanting her advice on running a fundraiser for the local animal shelter, and since she had so much experience with that sort of event blah, blah, blah. She was gracious enough to agree to see me, and I hung up, certain my karma would suffer from all of this deceitfulness.

After spending the better part of two hours on the phone, I signaled to Margo that I was taking a break. I headed out through the lobby, intent on taking a mug of coffee out into the sunshine for a few minutes, remembered the protestors, and redirected my steps toward the coat room and the blessed peace of the reading room beyond. Millie Haines came through the front door, ear glued to her cell phone, as always. I waved, intending to walk on by her, but to my surprise, she put a hand over the phone and mouthed, "Wait just a sec, okay?" She dispatched her caller within a few seconds and promptly turned her phone off. "Well, hey! Look at us two days from the end of the month with a few minutes to say hello to each other like real human beings. I feel as if we've hardly had a chance to get acquainted, and it's been nearly two months!"

I shifted uncomfortably, thwarted in my desire to escape to the reading room. No way to do that with Millie right there in my face, the intelligent brown eyes fringed in long lashes anxious to make nice. Might as well make the best of it, I decided, sighing inwardly. "Has it really been that long?" I responded with a half-hearted smile, my eyes straying over her shoulder into the coat room. "How is it going for you so far? Are you finding Connecticut to your liking?"

"It's a change from California, that's for sure." The way she said it, it sounded like "fer sher." An aging Valley Girl, I wondered? "I could do without all the humidity in the summer. Thank goodness for air conditioning, huh? But I'm just blown away by these autumn colors. I've never seen anything like it. Are the trees always so beautiful?"

For a moment, I couldn't think what she meant, and then I realized that Millie Haines was one of those rare creatures, a native Californian, who had never before experienced a New England autumn. I tried to imagine that and couldn't. It was like trying to imagine being blind. "Why, yes, pretty much. I mean, they're not always the same. It depends on how much water is in the ground when the hours of sunlight start decreasing and things like that, but it's always beautiful. This year, the trees have been especially vivid. I guess they're putting on a show to impress you."

"Well, they're doing a great job of it." She grinned, and for a second, she reminded me strongly of someone, but I couldn't quite think who.

"So you lived in California all your life?"

"Born and raised in the Napa Valley. If you have any questions about California wines, consider me your source. I was raised in wine country. I think the stuff runs in my veins, which is funny, because I can't drink more than one glass without falling sound asleep."

I chuckled. "I know what you mean, and that situation doesn't improve with age, believe me. I love the taste of good wine, but one glass, and it's 'night, night, Kate'. What made you decide to change coasts, Millie?"

She shrugged. "Middle-aged crisis, I guess. I was pushing forty-five and felt stuck in a rut, needed to shake myself up a little. A mortgage broker can do business anywhere—have phone, will travel. So I decided to take a look at the Atlantic Ocean, and here I am. By the way, I really wanted to mention how much I like your Emma. You must have done something awfully right for her to turn out to be such a peach, Kate, and so good at what she does. I don't know what my clients would do without her. They all just love her to pieces."

This was music to a mother's ears, of course, and I warmed to the woman on the spot. Obviously, she was both intelligent *and* perceptive. "How nice of you to say so," I murmured, trying unsuccessfully to appear modest.

"Anyway," Millie chirped, "gotta go, but I just wanted to take a minute to say hello, at least!" She turned the phone in her hand back on, and it rang immediately. "Bye now!" And off she went, leaving me standing in the middle of the lobby with my cooling coffee. A glance at my watch confirmed that I had been away from the phone for too long already, and reluctantly, I returned to the office to let Margo off the hook for a few minutes.

By 8:30, we were both exhausted. Margo could no longer put off Rhett, who was whining for his overdue dinner, and my brain was oatmeal. By mutual consent, we packed it in and dragged our bulging briefcases out to the lobby, which was lit only by the lamp on Jenny's desk. I poked my head into the stairwell and listened for Emma, but all was silent, and her car was gone from the curb when we walked out into the night. I remembered to mention my appointment with Mavis Griswold and begged Margo to recruit Jenny and cover the office for me when I went to the rectory the next afternoon. The thought of it filled me with dread.

"If Abby Stoddard wasn't such a really decent person," I grumped, "I never would have agreed to do this. I *hate* snooping. I don't want to know other people's secrets."

"I know what you mean, Hon. I can hardly bear up under the weight of my own past sins without havin' to deal with anybody else's messes." Rhett whined softly, and she patted his head. "You've been a darlin' to wait for your dinner this long. I'm gonna take you home right now and feed you up properly." Rhett panted happily, and they headed for the BMW, while I let myself into the Altima. A final tootle of the horn, and they were off. As the BMW's taillights receded in the distance, I became aware of how dark the night sky was and how deserted the street. The click of a man's heels sounded somewhere nearby. I shivered, not entirely with the cold, and quickly shut and locked my car door.

Traffic was light at that hour, and the ride home took only a few minutes. I was surprised, but glad, to see Manny's car in my driveway. At least Jasmine and Simon would have been fed, and if I was very lucky, dinner would be waiting for me, as well. Things were looking up.

"Hello!" I called, letting myself into the kitchen, but there was no answer. The cats' dish on the floor by the window had obviously been recently emptied, but the stove was cold, and the big, wooden salad bowl was empty. No wine, no candles, no nothing. Instantly, my mood soured. "Huh!" I said to nobody and thumped my briefcase and handbag down on the counter before hanging up my coat in the hall closet. Manny's jacket had been tossed over the back of a kitchen chair.

"Anybody home?" I tried again, heading for the family room, where the blaring television signaled Manny's presence. The man seemed incapable of existing in a silent room or car. The first thing he did when he entered either one was to turn something on. As I came into the room, both cats looked up at me sleepily from where they were curled snugly next to Manny, one on each side. It was clear that their bellies had been filled, and the TV didn't seem to bother them a bit. The light of my life lay sprawled in the big recliner chair, mouth agape, snoring gently. Frankly, it wasn't a good look for him.

"Hey!" I said loudly. "I'm home." No response. I plucked the remote control from his slack hand and clicked off the TV. Instantly, his eyes opened, and his fingers clutched reflexively for the missing remote. He stared uncomprehendingly at the dark TV before looking around to see me sitting on the sofa with my legs crossed, remote dangling from one hand.

"What time is it?" he asked groggily, and I tapped my watch with a fingernail.

"Nearly 9:00. Have a nice evening?" My foot twitched back and forth with annoyance. Would a sandwich have been too much to ask? Surely, he didn't think I was going to cook for him at this hour.

"Oh, my, I was totally out of it. I must have been really tired." He yawned widely. "How was your day?"

He was tired? I had left the house before 7:30 this

morning and had consumed only two cups of coffee and half a container of cold soup all day. "My day was long, that's how it was, and now I need some food and a hot bath so I can get up tomorrow and do it all over again," I snapped. I stood up and tossed the remote into his lap, startling Jasmine. Back in the kitchen, I yanked open the refrigerator door and began rummaging. A package of not-quite-thawed ground meat sat on the top shelf, and some limp veggies languished in the bin. I picked up the meat and stood staring at it stupidly, too weary to think what to do with it. Manny came into the kitchen behind me and pushed the refrigerator door shut, taking the package out of my hand. Deftly, he slid the cork out of a bottle of Australian Shiraz on the counter, poured a small glass, and put a handful of wheat crackers from their canister into a napkin. He handed me the glass and the napkin and turned me toward the hall.

"Have your bath, *Mia*," he said, "but don't fall asleep in the tub. Get into bed, and I will bring you a tray in a little while. Go, go!" He made shooing motions.

Too tired to argue, I went.

Ten minutes later, submerged to my chin in fragrant bubbles and the worst of my hunger held at bay by the crackers in my tummy, I sipped my wine in a much more positive frame of mind. The bathroom room stood open a couple of inches, and a very appetizing aroma wafted in from the kitchen. I caught myself just before I nodded off and emerged from the soothing suds reluctantly. I pulled one of Joey's old football jerseys over my head and slid between the sheets just as Manny arrived bearing dinner on a tray. I sniffed appreciatively at the two bowls that steamed under my nose as he pulled a wing chair next to my bed. He had added some diced potatoes to the meat, chopped up the limp vegetables, added a dash of the Shiraz and some spices and let everything simmer together. *Could there be nutmeg in there?* The stale Portuguese rolls he had found in the bread drawer had been sliced in half and slathered with olive oil and onion salt, then toasted for a few minutes. A big bunch of green grapes and a chunk of jack cheese completed the menu. Greedily, I grabbed a spoon and dug in while Manny settled into the wing chair. He tucked a napkin tidily into his collar before he helped himself to the remaining bowl of stew or goulash or whatever it was. For a few minutes, we ate in a companionable silence broken only by the chink of spoons on pottery. By the time I reached for the grapes, I felt almost human, my previous exhaustion replaced by a pleasant lassitude. Simon and Jasmine had come looking for us and lay curled up together at my feet. It might not be everyone's idea of a family, but it worked for me.

"So," Manny asked for the second time, "how was your day?"

This time, I answered him civilly. "Let's just say it ended up a whole lot better than it began." He served himself a few grapes and a piece of cheese while I filled him in on my unsettling conversation with Emma, whom Manny adored. He called her "Her Serene Highness," because of what he called her princess profile, and she called him Stepdaddy, only partly in jest. Now, his brow furrowed as he heard about Emma's refusal to explain her payoff to Prudence Crane. He reached out to take my hand in his.

"Do you think she needs our help?" was his first comment, and I smiled at him. How like him to cut right to what was important. What dreadful thing Emma might have done, or to whom she might have done it, were simply insignificant compared to the possibility that his princess might need rescuing. *First things first.*

"If she does, she knows where to find us," I reassured him. "In the meantime, I have to figure out a way to avoid having suspicion pointed at her, and that means finding out who really murdered dear Prudy." I sighed as I remembered my upcoming interview with the minister's wife the following day.

Wisely, Manny stayed out of it. "And if you need my help, you know where to find me, am I correct?" He released my hand and got to his feet. "And now I will leave you to your sleep." He picked up the reloaded tray and bent to kiss me. Feeling warm and cozy and loved, I took his handsome face between my hands and rubbed the end of his nose with my own.

"Eskimo kiss. Thank you for my delicious dinner—and for feeding the felines." I gave him a proper kiss and tried to pinch his backside, but he was too quick for me. He dodged my hand nimbly and backed out of the room, laughing. I switched off my bedside lamp and slid deeper under the covers, listening to him rattling dishes into the dishwasher for a few minutes. Is there a more welcome sound, I wondered sleepily, than listening to someone else do the dishes? I could definitely get used to it.

"Sleep well, *Cara*," he called softly down the hall. The lights went out, and then I heard the click of the kitchen door as he let himself into the garage. Immediately, I missed him and felt bad about his thirty-minute drive home to West Hartford. We really should move in together, I thought. And then I fell into a dead sleep.

Six

Thursday was yet another impossibly gorgeous day. *Too bad I can't enjoy it.* I groused to myself and tried to distract myself from my upcoming interview with Mavis Griswold by dealing with the accumulated paperwork of the week. At the appointed hour, I left Margo on the phones, Rhett Butler lolling at her feet, and walked the two long blocks down Old Main Street to the white clapboard church.

Across the street, a pod of protestors paced silently outside the Keeney Memorial, cigarettes dangling from their mouths and fingers. The poster-board signs they held aloft proclaimed, with various levels of spelling success, their unhappiness about the proposed smoking ban in the old business district. The uproar had prompted the Village Business Association to schedule a public hearing the following Monday evening, and debate promised to be spirited.

As I approached the corner of Church Street, I looked up at the spire of the old edifice, appreciating its clean, white lines against the blue sky. Behind the church was the ancient burying ground where half the town's forefathers lay, presumably at peace, in graves dating back a century or more. Most of the names etched on the monuments and headstones were still readable. They included many I recognized, if only from local street names. It was difficult to imagine a more peaceful vista. It seemed incredible that I was about to knock on the door of the residence and ask the minister's wife, with whom I was barely acquainted, if she had an alibi for the night of Prudy Crane's murder, but there it was. The police were nipping at Abby's heels, my daughter was involved in something so dreadful she couldn't tell me about it, and however reluctantly, I was investigating a murder. Again. *It's a good thing I don't write mystery novels. I couldn't make this stuff up.*

The sheltered flower beds that flanked the residence's door were still fragrant with blooms, and a few late summer bees bumbled among them and enjoyed their bounty. I let the ornate brass knocker fall against its backplate. Looking every inch the proper minister's wife in a dark blue shirtdress, low heels and pearls, gray hair pinned into a smooth bun at the nape of her neck, Mavis Griswold opened the door promptly. Her smile was gracious, and I returned it as warmly as I could. "Thank you for seeing me, Mrs. Griswold. I know how busy you are."

"Not at all, my dear. Do come in and make yourself comfortable," she invited. She led me down the wide center hall to a cozy study at the back of the house overlooking a tidy back yard and the cemetery beyond. Fresh flowers filled a cut glass bowl on a coffee table between two Queen Anne chairs slip-covered in a rosy print. They faced each other in front of a diminutive fireplace. Next to the flowers sat a china tea service, obviously a cherished heirloom, and two impossibly thin cups and saucers. "I thought you might enjoy a cup of tea with me. I generally have one about this time." She gestured to one of the chairs, and I sat, feeling large and clumsy amid the dainty furnishings, while she seated herself and poured out a cup of fragrant herb tea. Cinnamon something, I thought, wrinkling my nose appreciatively. "Lemon? Milk?"

"Just a little sugar, please." I accepted the proffered cup and stirred my tea silently as I struggled to find a way to begin. "Mrs. Griswold, I'm sure you were surprised at my call yesterday, since we don't know each other and I'm not a member of your church. The truth is, I'm not here to talk about running a fundraiser, but I preferred to tell you the real reason for my visit in person." I took an unladylike gulp of my tea. "The fact is, I'm here at the request of Abigail Stoddard in connection with the murder of Prudence Crane. Abby is aware that Prudy was blackmailing you, but she prefers not to share that information with the police unless she absolutely must. We are both hoping that you will discuss this with me so that we can eliminate you as a suspect, rather than suggesting you as one to the police. I assure you that both Abby and I can be trusted. Whatever you choose to tell me will be held in complete confidence."

I had expected shock, anger, or perhaps stammered denials. What I got was none of the above. For a long moment, Mavis sat gazing at me through her long fringe of eyelashes, the sweet smile undimmed. Her brown eyes were tranquil, and I was reminded yet again of a friendly cow.

"I've been wondering if anyone would come to ask me those questions," she commented matter of fact, as if I had just asked her where she bought her groceries. "I just didn't know it would be you." Then she put down her cup and rose to look out of the window. It had been raised a few inches to let in the sweet, autumn air.

"It will seem off the point, I'm sure, and your not being from around here may make it more difficult. You see, I really can't answer you question until I tell you a bit about Harriet Wheeler." She looked back over her shoulder at me. "Have you even heard that name before?"

I had. "Being in the real estate business, I've learned quite a bit about many of the older homes in Wethersfield, Mrs. Griswold. If I remember correctly, Mrs. Wheeler owned one of the lovely Victorians on Wolcott Hill Road. She was something of a local celebrity—a writer, I think—until her death last winter. Have I got it right?"

Mavis nodded and turned back to the window. "Harriett Wheeler was widowed at the beginning of World War II. She wrote a couple of dozen romance novels, very prim, not like the ones you find out there today, that were quite popular years ago. She also raised a daughter, Sarah, by herself. It was just the two of them in that rambling old house. The day after Sarah graduated from high school in 1960, she took off for the West Coast, and nobody seemed to know for certain what happened to Sarah after that. There was a rumor that she had married a man in California and they had both been killed soon thereafter in an automobile accident."

I sipped some tea and refrained from interrupting.

"The royalties from Mrs. Wheeler's books allowed her to live out her years in comfort, although nobody saw much of her. She preferred to live in semi-seclusion, tending to her perennial borders, surrounded by her books and music. She died as she had lived, quietly and without a fuss. The rumors of her daughter's death seemed to be confirmed when Harriett left her house to her neighbor, Will Copeland, a local firefighter who had helped Harriett out over the years. He took care of the lawn and shoveled the snow and generally maintained the exterior of the property.

"Having struggled to raise and educate four children on a fireman's salary, Will and his wife were delighted with their good fortune. They lost no time converting the house into two flats, upstairs and downstairs. They rented the smaller, upstairs unit to Prudy Crane while they worked on restoring the first floor to its original glory. That part was a real labor of love. They planned to sell their house next door and move into the downstairs of the Wheeler house themselves."

Mavis returned to the chair opposite me and picked up her cooling tea. "As a part of all this, Will worked for weeks to clean out the cavernous cellar where Harriett had kept, along with her personal papers, every word of every draft she had ever written. The back porch of the old house was stacked with cartons waiting for the recycler. Prudy being Prudy, she snooped through them all. In one of them, she found Harriett's personal diaries, which recounted in detail a high school relationship between Harriett's daughter Sarah and a local minister's son. Very soon thereafter, Prudy started demanding money from me."

I hadn't seen that one coming. "But why? What did you have to do with any of what you've just told me?"

"My maiden name was Sarah Mavis Wheeler," she replied. "Harriett Wheeler was my mother. Apparently, my youthful indiscretions were all laid out for Prudy in Mother's old diaries. She was a compulsive chronicler. More tea?"

"Not just yet, thanks," I said, astounded by this revelation. I struggled to straighten out my face as Mavis returned to her chair.

Mavis sat back and continued her story, her eyes occasionally distant as she reached back into her memories. "My husband Henry, who is now the minister here, succeeded his father in that position. When Henry Senior held the post, my Henry was in high school with me right here in Wethersfield all those years ago, and we fell in love. The fact is, we had a love affair of the sort Mother never would have written about, I'm afraid. Of course, I got pregnant." She crossed her ankles and clasped her hands loosely in her lap, every inch the composed matron. "Fortunately, I was only weeks from graduating when I found out, so I was allowed to remain here long enough to get my diploma. But the very next day, I was banished to a facility in California, where I stayed until I had the baby, a little girl, and gave it up for adoption.

I found my voice at last. "And then you came home?"

Her smile was bitter this time. "Oh, that might have been possible in another place and time, but as I've said,

Wethersfield is a very small town, and it was the '60s. My ruined virtue became common knowledge, and Mother simply could not bear the shame of it all. Had it been a different time, a different place, Henry and I would have made different choices, but at the time, my disappearing and giving up our daughter was presented to us as the only option. Mother was a very forceful personality. She forbade me to return, if you can believe it." Her mouth twisted in remembered pain.

My heart went out to her. "How terrible for you. What did you do? Did you have any friends or relatives to turn to out there?"

"No, no one. Everyone on both sides of our family lived right here in provincial New England. California may as well have been China. But somehow I managed. I was eighteen by then and got a job as a clerk at the state university in San Jose. After I established a year's residence, I was entitled to free tuition at a state institution, so I put myself through school and got a better job. I lost a lot of weight, dyed my hair brown, and got contact lenses to replace my eyeglasses. Then I went to probate court and changed my name legally to Mavis Wellman. My transformation was complete. As far as people in Wethersfield knew, Sarah Wheeler had disappeared."

"Who started the rumor that you were killed in a car crash out west? What happened to Henry all that time?" By now, I was completely caught up in Mavis' story.

"To answer your first question, probably Mother herself. She never got over the horror of having an unwed mother for a daughter. It was far preferable to tell people that I had died, which made her a tragic figure instead of a mean old woman, which is what she really was, you know. As for Henry, he suffered in his own way. The shame wasn't as bad for his family, of course. Even ministers' boys will be boys, and you know the old double standard. So they just packed him off to a seminary in Oregon, trusting that he would get over his little crush. But in reality, we were always in contact, writing and calling, even visiting each other when he got a break from his studies. When he was ordained, he took a posting in northern California instead of going back East. In 1981, when his father was nearing retirement, Henry was invited to fill the position of senior minister. Since people's memories had faded and my appearance had been sufficiently altered, I married him and returned not as Sarah Wheeler but as Henry's bride Mavis, recently of California. So we eventually worked out a happy ending to our story, but it wasn't tidy enough for Mother. Real life seldom is, I find."

I was quiet, imagining myself in Mavis' situation all those years ago. What would I have done in her place? "Please forgive me for asking, but was it really so unthinkable for you to defy your mother? Even in 1960, unwed mothers weren't exactly being tarred and feathered, as I recall. If you and Henry were so very much in love, why couldn't you marry and raise your daughter—even if you were young and the baby arrived a bit early?"

Mavis didn't appear to take offense. She sipped her tea thoughtfully. "It simply didn't occur to me, I suppose. I was a placid sort of child, a pleaser, I guess you would say. I was seventeen years old, not yet of legal age, and defying Mother was no more an option for me than getting an abortion."

I winced at the parallel she had chosen to draw.

"Oh, yes, that crossed my mind. Another girl in my senior class who found herself in the same predicament had done just that. But I had been raised to believe that abortion is murder, all the more heinous because the victim is an unborn child. Henry felt the same way."

Mavis set down her cup and met my eyes. "I wonder if it's possible for you to understand. You and I don't know each other very well, I realize, but a minister's wife is accustomed to observing others. I've often seen you with your daughter… Emma, is it?… on your morning walks down to the cove or having coffee together at the diner. You're always nattering away or laughing about something. You seem very free and open with each other, more like girlfriends than mother and daughter. I don't imagine that there are many secrets between you."

My heart dropped as I remembered my last conversation with Emma. "Well, one or two, perhaps," I protested weakly. "Everyone has secrets, especially from their parents. But generally speaking, Emma and I can talk about most things." *Except why she was spotted paying off a known blackmailer. Apparently, that topic is off limits.* To cover my confusion, I held out my cup for a refill. What a fraud I was, sitting here questioning Mavis' long-ago choices and allowing myself to be mistaken for a model mother.

Mavis tipped the old teapot over my cup, replenishing the fragrant brew. The incongruity of our surroundings and our conversation struck me. Here we were in this charming old parsonage, two ladies chatting over our teacups—about blackmail, abortion, and yes… murder. All those straitlaced parishioners in the burying ground behind us must be aghast.

I dragged my attention back to the topic at hand. "Please know that my openness with Emma doesn't mean I can't understand your situation. My relationship with my own mother was guarded, to say the least."

Mavis nodded understandingly. "I'm sure. That was the way it was when you and I were young." Her eyes grew distant once again. "In my case, it was ridiculous to think the truth would never come out, of course. It always does, and its potential to do damage escalates exponentially with the passage of time. Our story was no exception. By the time Prudy got hold of it, Henry's parents were long dead, but he and Mother and I had been living a lie for more than forty years. Precisely because it had been kept secret for all that time, our adolescent peccadillo would have achieved the status of a full-blown scandal, one that would totally overshadow Henry's decades of selfless service to the church and the community, just as he was looking forward to retirement. I simply couldn't let Prudy do it to him, to us."

I swallowed hard. "Are you telling me you killed her, Mrs. Griswold?"

Mavis' eyebrows climbed her forehead. "Why, no," she replied calmly. "Oh, I wouldn't be human if I didn't admit that it crossed my mind. Helping Prudence Crane to meet her Maker could almost be considered an act of compassion. She wasn't only my cross to bear, after all.

She made the lives of everyone with whom she came into contact a living hell. But," she smiled almost impishly, "the good Lord apparently saw fit to assign the task to someone else."

I believed her. It was impossible to look into those serene brown eyes and do anything else. I put my empty teacup on the coffee table and groped for my handbag at my feet. "Thank you for speaking with me so frankly, Mrs. Griswold. You certainly didn't have to, but you've helped me enormously. I only hope our conversation hasn't been too distressing for you."

"Mrs. Griswold is a bit formal under the circumstances, don't you think? Please call me Mavis. And on the contrary, I can't tell you what a relief it's been to confide in someone after all these years," she reassured me as we headed for the study door. "I'm really most grateful to you, my dear."

I could understand her feelings. After decades of allowing others to unburden themselves to her, of keeping their secrets and offering advice, the relief of finally sharing her own story must be exquisite. "Please know that what you've told me this afternoon will go no further unless that becomes absolutely necessary, and at this moment, I can't think why it would." I frowned as something occurred to me. "Mavis, do you happen to know what else was in your mother's diaries?"

"Quite a bit, I would imagine. Mother didn't miss much," she said drily.

"Haven't you seen them?"

"Why, no, I haven't. Mother and I weren't close enough for her to acknowledge my existence. She left her house to her neighbor. She would scarcely entrust her diaries to me."

Good point. "Do you have any idea what happened to them after Prudy got her hands on them?"

Mavis thought a bit. "I suppose the police must have them. Isn't it routine in these matters for the authorities to search the victim's home for clues?"

I considered this. "The police couldn't have the diaries, or they'd be the ones questioning you instead of me."

"Then Prudy must have hidden them somewhere," Mavis concluded quite logically. "But where?"

"There are too many people at the diner for her to have found a safe hiding place there. They have to be in your mother's house somewhere, just not in Prudy's apartment. Remember, the police don't know these diaries exist, so they're not looking for them. Do you have any idea? Did you have a secret hiding place in that house when you were a child?"

Mavis shook her head regretfully. "I was a very timid child. There's a huge attic, but the bats and the squirrels frightened me, and I avoided the big, dark basement at all costs."

The prospect of searching those spaces didn't do much for me, either. "I don't know how I'm going to do it yet, but if I'm going to have a chance of figuring this situation out, I have to find those diaries. When I do, what shall I do with them?"

"Why, you must do whatever you think best, dear. I leave it entirely in your capable hands." Mavis smiled serenely. "I have faith."

~ * ~

Late that afternoon, I finished returning phone calls and trudged up the stairs to the loft to fill Emma in on my conversation with Mavis Griswold. She switched the phones to the answering machine and led me into her phantom boss's office, closing the door behind us. She listened to my tale without interruption. "But how are you going to get into the Wheeler house?" she asked. The Copelands aren't living there yet, but they own the property. Prudy's apartment must still be sealed by the police. Short of breaking and entering, I really don't see how—"

She was interrupted by someone pounding on Jimmy's door, and then Margo burst into the room followed closely by Rhett Butler. "Hey, ladies, what's cookin'?" She plopped into the second guest chair and beamed at us both. Rhett trotted directly to Emma, whom he adored almost as much as Margo, and put his head in her lap. Emma smiled at Rhett and scratched his head.

"Later," I said. "What happened with Lieutenant Harkness?"

"In front of the child?" Margo asked, feigning shock while she kicked off her Manolos and wiggled her stockinged toes.

Emma rolled her eyes. "Give."

I nodded my agreement.

Torn between his two loves, Rhett walked to the middle of the room and flopped down on the floor at a point precisely midway between Margo and Emma, panting happily.

"Well, if you insist. Would either one of you happen to have a piece of gum?"

I threw my purse at her, while Emma tossed the box of tissues from Jimmy's desk.

"Okay, okay! Here's what I know so far. It's not much, because the delectable lieutenant only had a few minutes for me. The mayor was expectin' him, you see," she offered by way of explanation.

"Hardnose kept the mayor waiting while he talked with you?" Emma asked in disbelief.

Margo smiled at her kindly. "Why, yes. He's such a gentleman, don't you think?" She smoothed her linen sheath over her slim thighs and admired the result.

"Not according to Rick Fletcher or any of the other young cops on the force," Emma snorted. "Rick says he's a complete—"

"Stop it!" I hissed at the two of them. "Emma, be quiet now, and Margo, I swear, if you don't tell me what you found out right this minute…"

It was Margo's turn to roll her eyes, but "Okey dokey," was all she said. "First, I introduced myself and explained that as a local realtor with listings in the area of the old Wheeler house I very naturally had an interest in how visible any ongoing investigation of the premises might be, not wanting to spook any potential buyers. I must say John was very understandin'."

"John?" Emma interrupted, and I quelled her with a look.

Margo smiled again. "Yes, John understood my concerns perfectly. He went out of his way to explain that the crime unit had already completed a very thorough investigation of Prudy's apartment, dustin' for fingerprints and takin' up the carpets, lookin' for fibers and hairs and all that sort of disgustin' forensic evidence. It was their belief that not only did Prudy live alone, but she couldn't have had any visitors, either. The crime lab technicians spent a lot of time goin' over every little thing, and they didn't turn up one single piece of evidence that any other person had ever set foot in her apartment. Isn't that just the weirdest thing you ever heard?"

Emma and I stared at her. "I can't believe Hardnose gave up that much information to someone outside the department on five minutes' acquaintance," I said finally.

"Two minutes, Sugar," Margo said smugly. "The mayor was waitin', remember. Anyway, the point is that the forensic investigation of Prudy's apartment appears to be complete. The crime scene tape is still in place, but John said that the new owners are free to come and go now."

I chewed over what Margo had learned. "Did Hardnose mention finding any diaries at Prudy's place?" I gave her a short version of the interview I had had with Mavis Griswold earlier that afternoon.

Margo listened closely, her eyes half closed while she processed what I had to say. "Elsie the Cow had a calf? Amazin'. No, John didn't mention any diaries, but I'll raise the question with him again later. We're havin' dinner this evenin'."

Emma choked in disbelief, but I waved off any comment. "Good. But if they have the diaries, then why haven't they questioned Mavis…?"

"…and if they don't have them, how did they know Prudy was blackmailing Abby?" Margo finished my thought.

"Good point," I agreed, and Emma nodded.

"We still haven't solved the problem of how we're going to get into Prudy's apartment to search it ourselves—unless, of course, John handed over a key to the place," she joked.

If possible, Margo looked even more smug. "Not a problem, girlfriends. The good lieutenant let it slip that the Copelands have decided to dump the Wheeler house. Can't stand the idea of living with a murder victim's ghost or some such twaddle. At any rate, they want out, the sooner the better. I know it was tacky of me, but I simply couldn't help myself. I ran right over to see them." She risked her manicure by scrabbling in the bottom of her Etienne Aigner tote. She produced a set of huge, old fashioned keys, which she dangled before us tantalizingly. "And guess who's got the listin'!"

Seven

Usually, I anticipated Fridays with pleasure, but today wasn't one of those days. I had been looking forward to spending Thursday evening with Armando, but an unexpected software problem at work had caused him to cancel our dinner date. I had consoled myself with half a bottle of wine and wound up tossing and turning all night, to the annoyance of Jasmine and Simon. They retreated to the family room sofa in the wee hours, and I fell into a sleep too restless to be restorative. I awoke with a headache at 6:00 and grumped off to meet Emma for a walk before work, hoping some exercise would perk me up. It didn't.

A cold fog had rolled off the Connecticut River and enveloped Old Wethersfield from its banks nearly to the Silas Deane Highway. The water of the cove was barely visible, disappearing into the swirling mist just a few feet from shore. Even the birds were silent. By unspoken agreement, we avoided the diner, grabbing coffee to go from Dory's on our way back up the hill, and at the corner of Church Street, we crossed Old Main, giving a wide berth to the spot where we had found Prudy's body. The scarecrows in front of the Blades Salon had been totally dismantled. Jay and Ed, the owners, had filled the awkward gap with some artfully arranged wheat sheaves, pumpkins and mums. To out-of-town tourists, the new display probably looked fine, but it only served to remind us locals of what had been in its place.

Margo had talked the Copelands into scheduling an open house on Sunday. Will and Janet were eager to divest themselves of what they now considered to be a white elephant, but Margo considered it a lucrative opportunity. "The curiosity factor alone will bring people out in record numbers," she predicted. "Nothin' folks like better than a chance to gawk at a crime scene. And once they see how nice it is inside, we're just bound to find a buyer. If we keep a sharp eye out, we can see what other locals show up who might be considered suspects. With any luck at all, we'll solve this little mystery and make a tidy profit, too!"

I had my doubts about how profitable this listing would turn out to be, but my main interest was getting inside the place to hunt for Harriett Wheeler's diaries. Grace Sajak and her crew had been dispatched to remove the crime scene tape, vacuum and clean the fingerprinting dust, and generally remove any remaining traces of the police investigation of Prudy's apartment. We trusted Grace absolutely, and she knew not to relocate anything. As squeamish as the Copelands now were about the property, they were only too happy to leave the preparations to Margo and me. Along with Emma, we planned to take full advantage of our access on Saturday. In the meantime, there was today to get through.

"So what's on your sleuthing agenda today?" Emma asked as we trudged toward the Law Barn. It being the last day of the month, she would be flat out all day handling closings.

I considered my options. The last thing I felt like doing was prying into yet another family's personal business, but it had to be done if we were to get Abby off the hook. Since our meeting, Abby had scrupulously avoided contacting me, but I knew she had to be anxious for news. "First, I want to hear what Margo learned from John Harkness last night."

Emma smirked. "I have a feeling he learned a thing or two from Margo, too."

I shot her a look but decided to overlook her implication. My head wasn't up to a quarrel this early in the day. "Then, if the police don't appear to have Harriett Wheeler's diaries, we'll have to contact the Copelands and fabricate a reason to get some time alone in that house to search for them." I sighed. "And last but not least, I have to make an appointment to talk with Ephraim Marsh. Whoever else may be mentioned in Harriett's diaries, we already know that Prudy was blackmailing Ephraim." My head throbbed at the thought of another awkward interview.

Emma was silent for a moment as we walked along. Then, "I might be able to help you out there. That is," she amended somewhat diffidently for her, "if you think I should."

I dragged my eyes up from the sidewalk to search her face. "How do you mean?"

"I've met the Marshes before. Remember, Joey and I

went to school in Newington, and the Newington kids and the Wethersfield kids all hung out together. Big football rivals. There were always big parties after the games, and we went to each other's mixers, you remember."

I nodded.

"Anyway, I know Amy Marsh, his daughter. I went to a couple of parties at her house when we were in high school, met her parents. I haven't seen Amy for years, but every now and then, I'd run into her Thanksgiving weekend at the homecoming game when she was home from college visiting her folks like everyone else."

More likely, they ran into each other at a bar in Hartford, I thought. Local tradition called for the younger alumni to barhop on Thanksgiving night to blow off some steam after a long, full day with their relatives. It was the only time many of them got to catch up with each other after they graduated from high school and dispersed to jobs and colleges all over the country. As did most of the other old fogies, I understood the custom without condoning it.

"So I remember one Thanksgiving night about three years ago. A bunch of us, including Amy, met up at City Steam and decided it would be a hoot to go up on Cedar Mountain to our old hangout, build a bonfire, drink some beer, you know." She glanced sideways at me.

I knew what she meant all too well. Emma had been quite the wild child for a few years following her father's and my divorce, and a lot more than beer drinking had gone on at those woodland get-togethers. We both had some painful memories of those days, but I kept mine to myself for the moment.

"I don't understand how that helps me to get Ephraim to open up to me," I said cautiously. "'My daughter used to go drinking with your daughter' doesn't strike me as a big confidence-inspirer."

Emma had the grace to look uncomfortable. "The thing is, something happened that night. I hadn't thought about it for a long while, but it popped into my head yesterday, and I think it might be important."

I tried to look encouraging without being nosy, a trick I had never quite mastered.

Emma continued. "Amy fell that night, badly. We had all had a few beers, and we were stumbling up the mountain in the dark. Everybody was laughing and shushing each other and walking into trees... and then Amy yelped and went down on both knees. For a few seconds, we tried to pull her back up on her feet, but she started screaming and crying. Then we knew she was really hurt. It was bad."

I pictured the scene in my mind, a dozen or so tipsy young people crashing around in the woods on Cedar Mountain in the dark. It wasn't surprising that someone had been hurt. "What did you do?"

Emma got a faraway look in her eyes, remembering. "It was a tough spot. We had all been drinking, and we didn't want to call the cops at first. But then we remembered that we were all of legal drinking age, not like the old days." She stopped and chewed her lip, but I let it pass without comment. "So I got out my cell phone and called Joey, and he remembered that Rick Fletcher was on the job, so he called him, and Rick called a buddy on the Newington force, and, well, they fixed it."

I looked directly at her for the first time since she had started this story. "Fixed it?"

Hearing it come out of my mouth, Emma realized how that sounded. "Oh, no, not 'fixed it' the way you mean it. They didn't do anything illegal. It just so happened that Rick was off duty that night, so he got his buddy from Newington, and they came up the old mountain road as far as they could in Rick's personal car, and then they walked in with a stretcher and big torches and carried Amy out."

"And took her where?"

"To the emergency room, of course! She had torn the tendons in her left knee. We all just thought it would be nicer for Amy's parents to think she had done it falling down the stairs at someone's house than walking into a tree, drunk. So Rick and his friend disappeared, and that's what we told them."

"Huh. Your brother never said a word to me. No wonder you and Rick Fletcher are so friendly. It's an interesting story, Em, but I doubt that Prudy could blackmail Amy's father with it."

"I haven't finished." Emma paused to choose her words as we turned into the Law Barn's driveway. "It was about a year later, I think. It might even have been the following Thanksgiving weekend, I can't remember. But for some reason, Amy's name came up, and we were talking about that night. Somebody said—and honestly, 'Cita, I don't remember who it was—that Amy's knee had given her a lot of trouble. They had to do a second surgery, and the physical therapy afterwards was very painful. The doctor prescribed a strong painkiller, Vico-something—"

"Vicodin."

"That's it, Vicodin. And Amy got so dependent on the stuff that she started helping herself to it out of her dad's pharmacy. She worked there part-time. I don't know for a fact that it's true, but if it was, that could mean big trouble for Mr. Marsh, right?"

"The worst," I agreed. I stopped at the entrance. "Aside from having a daughter who's an addict, which would certainly be trouble enough, Ephraim could lose his license. Vicodin is a narcotic, a controlled substance. He could be prosecuted, lose his business, everything." I put my hand on her arm for emphasis. "I'm glad you told me, Emma, but it absolutely cannot go any further."

"You know it won't, at least not from me. But if that's why Mr. Marsh was on Prudy's hook, somebody else must have told her, Momma."

There was that name again, another bad omen on an already gloomy morning.

Emma disappeared up the stairs to her loft, and after checking to be sure Jenny's back was to me, I tiptoed to the Reading room to wash my face and regroup. Moving quietly to the left end of the coat rack, I pressed the paneling, and the door popped open half an inch with an almost inaudible click. Checking over my shoulder one more time, I slipped my fingers into the crack and let myself in. Once inside, I used the decorative pull cord on that side of the door to pull it shut. I splashed some cold water on my face, and swallowed two Advils from the bottle we kept in the cupboard under the sink, then switched on the table lamp and sank into the overstuffed chair to review what Emma had told me about the Marshes.

It was dispiriting, to say the least. I had been having my prescriptions filled at the pharmacy, and the homey, old-time atmosphere of the place took me back to my childhood in the '50s. Back then, a quarter would buy you a hot fudge sundae, with three scoops of ice cream and real whipped cream, at the counter in Nelson's Drugstore. Marsh's didn't have a counter, of course, but the feel of the place was the same. The wooden floor boards creaked cozily under your feet, and the magazine rack reminded me of Nelson's comic book stand. Ephraim Marsh himself stood behind the prescription counter much of the time, backed up by two young graduates of the U Conn School of Pharmacy and a couple of part-time clerks, who divided the store's thirteen-hour days among them. Though it wasn't really expected anymore, Ephraim still wore a crisp, white smock on duty, no doubt freshly laundered by his good wife Betsy. On the few occasions I had seen Ephraim and Betsy together, they had looked happy. I rubbed my throbbing temples. Was I going to be the one to put an end to their contentment, perhaps ruin the rest of their lives?

I was jolted out of my reverie by Jenny's voice, which resonated in my left ear as clearly as if she were standing next to me. "Hey, Margo! How's it going?" I grabbed the arms of the chair and leaned forward.

"Not too bad, Jenny," Margo answered her just as clearly. "Always good on a Friday, right, Darlin'?" Jenny laughed in answer, and I heard every nuance of her giggle. Wildly, I looked around me. Could they be in the coatroom on the other side of the wall? I held my breath and waited. Months ago, Margo and I had checked to be sure the light from the lamp wasn't visible under the door hidden in the paneling, so I wasn't worried about that, but where were the voices coming from?

A telephone rang, and Jenny answered it, somewhat farther removed from her original position. "Law Barn, Jenny speaking. How may I help you?" She had to be at her desk in the lobby, then. I resumed breathing, but how in the world was I hearing her? I had never heard anything from inside the reading room before. In fact, I assumed that it had been at least partially soundproofed so that those outside wouldn't hear water running from inside the room.

I sank back into the chair and looked around me more carefully. For the first time, I examined the elaborate pattern of the wallpaper that surrounded the door and covered the wall above the vanity. Beyond noticing that the floral print seemed too large for such a small room, I had never taken much note of it, but now I peered at it closely. The pattern featured blowsy cabbage roses of dark magenta set against a forest green background. The center of each flower was almost black, and it was from one of these, positioned slightly above the left arm of the chair in which I sat, that the sound seemed to emanate. Gently, I rubbed my fingers across it and was startled when a black disk of some kind dropped to the carpet. At the same time, Jenny's voice came through even more clearly as she laughed and chatted with a caller on the telephone. I picked up the lamp and held it above the arm of the chair. A round opening in the center of the cabbage rose became visible. It appeared to be a conduit of some kind. Cautiously, I picked up the object that had dropped to the floor and examined it. On closer inspection, it was made of rubber or soft plastic of some kind, wider at one end than at the other, and appeared to be made to fit into the opening in the wall. I experimented with it and found that by inserting the narrow end into the opening first, it became a perfectly fitted plug that projected only minutely from the wall when in place. Even more interestingly, it silenced the voices.

Suddenly, I understood. Mr. Watercolors, who had had this hiding place constructed, did more than startle his guests by disappearing and reappearing at his social gatherings. He used this diabolical listening device to *eavesdrop* on them from the comfort of his private den. In all this time, none of us had ever noticed the plug in the cabbage rose. I must have bumped it partially loose when I dropped into the chair this morning. I started to giggle, then clapped a hand over my mouth. If I could hear voices at this end of the tube, could I be heard at the other end? Then I remembered that the plug was back in place. But where was the other end of the conduit? I switched off the lamp and listened at the door to be sure the coast was clear, then scurried out into the coatroom. I could hardly wait to tell Margo and Emma about my discovery.

Barely flipping a wave to Jenny in passing, I bolted into the office and startled Margo, who was checking messages on our land line. "Psssst! Hey! Put that down," I hissed, flapping my hands at her. "You are not going to believe—"

She held up a warning hand and frowned into the receiver. "Hush!" Her frown deepened, and she reached for the pad and pencil next to the phone and began to make hurried notes. She scribbled furiously for another few seconds, while I tapped my foot impatiently, then finally put down the receiver. "Damn! The financing on the Hurlbut deal fell through at the last minute. There's a lien that should have been removed from the last re-fi. Is it eight thirty yet? Oh, good, it is! I just have time to nip over to the town hall and get this cleaned up before the closing."

"But wait—"

"Is Emma in yet? Oh, of course she is, it's the thirtieth. Listen, Sugar, be a pal and get Rhett into his pen, would you? I've got to dash upstairs." While she talked, she pulled a stuffed file folder out of her carryall, tore off the sheet of notepaper she'd been writing on, and handed Rhett's leash to me. He'd follow Margo anywhere without one, but he needed the extra encouragement of a tug on the leash to accompany anyone else. Margo flew out of the office, completely frustrating me.

It was awful to have such a juicy secret and no one to share it with. I stared at the dog who had not missed the transfer of authority his mistress had executed on her way out the door. I clipped the leash onto his collar, and he didn't bother making a fuss, just stood up and prepared to follow me wherever I led him.

I was tempted to hand Rhett over to Jenny and take advantage of her absence to try to locate the lobby end of the listening tube, but I knew that would be futile. The Law Barn phones were ringing off the hook today, and it wasn't fair to Jenny or our clients to take her away from her job. It would have to wait until two of the five of us who were in on the secret of the reading room had the time and privacy to pursue it. As eager as I was to solve this little mystery, another, more compelling puzzle was already on my agenda. I remembered that I hadn't asked

Margo what she'd learned from John Harkness the previous evening, either.

Resigning myself to waiting, I settled Rhett outside in his pen with a chew toy and a water dish. The sun was trying to come out, and he had a yard full of squirrels to enjoy. The lids were still on the trash cans, I noticed. Emma's peanuts had apparently had the desired effect on Fat Squirrel, who scolded me soundly from a maple bough that drooped over my head from the combined weight of F.S. and the bird feeder Emma had already begun filling for the winter ahead. Spilled seeds littered the ground, and I glared at him. No wonder we had mice. Still scolding, he fired a peanut shell at me, and I retreated to the relative peace of my office.

By midday, the phones had quieted down. The remaining closings, scheduled for this afternoon, were in Emma's hands now. Margo had apparently gone directly from the town hall to her closing this morning, since she hadn't reappeared. Feeling at loose ends and a little wired from all of the coffee I had consumed, I switched on MACK's answering service and left the building. The sun had finally broken through, burning off the cold mist of the morning, and a few tourists had ventured forth to admire the parade of scarecrows along Old Main Street. For once, the smoking ban protestors were not in evidence in front of the Keeney Memorial. Not knowing what else to do, I crossed the street and walked slowly toward Marsh's Pharmacy at the end of the block. I had no idea how to approach Ephraim. I only knew that for Abby's sake, I had to try. At least the information Emma had given me was a place to start.

The pharmacy, when I entered it, was quiet. Most of the historic district's business workers were at the diner or Dory's, or maybe the tea room, enjoying a bite of lunch. A couple of customers I didn't recognize were browsing among the cosmetics and toiletries, and Mort Delahanty stood at the magazine rack, thumbing through a copy of *Field & Stream* before his afternoon shift at the diner began. As always, Ephraim stood at the prescription counter in his starched, white smock, restocking the rows of vitamin supplements in the glass cases beneath the ancient cash register. One of his young pharmacists, a pretty young woman, was busy filling prescriptions at the other end of the work space, but no customers waited for attention. I swallowed hard and walked up next to Ephraim, my heart pounding.

"Ephraim?" He looked up from his work and smiled welcomingly. Thinning red hair framed a comfortably craggy face. He looked as honest and friendly as an old setter dog. "I don't know if you remember me. I'm Kate Lawrence from MACK Realty down the street. I need to discuss a personal matter with you. Would it be convenient for you to give me a few minutes now, or may I set an appointment for later in the day?"

He straightened up, managing to conceal any surprise he may have felt. "Why, hello, Kate. How have you been? I hear you've got a hot real estate market these days. Good for you!" He rubbed the small of his back. "Either these shelves are getting lower, or my back is getting creakier, but let's not go there," he said ruefully. "Sure, I've got some time right now, if you like. Ellie," he signaled to the pretty young pharmacist, "I'll be in the back room on a consultation. Just let me know if you need me."

"Sure thing, Ephraim, but it's pretty quiet right now. I'll take care of the phones."

I smiled and nodded to her as I followed Ephraim the few steps behind the partition that concealed his private workspace and accepted the straight chair he cleared off for me. No doubt he thought I was here to consult with him on some embarrassing medical problem, like hot flashes, or a scaly rash. I felt like the fraud I was and gulped audibly. "I guess I should say straight out that I'm not here for professional advice, Ephraim," I began, keeping my voice low. The partition that separated us from the register area didn't quite reach the store ceiling, and I didn't want to risk being overheard.

"Oh? What then?" he asked kindly, and I launched into my tale, just wanting to get it over with. I started by reminding him about the circumstances of Prudence Crane's death, then explained Abby Stoddard's dilemma, which was the real reason for my visit.

"Abby doesn't want to point a finger at anyone else, but the fact is, she may be arrested at any moment, and she knows for a fact that Prudy was blackmailing you. She saw you paying her off, Ephraim. You're not the only one she saw, but I need to know why, if only to eliminate you as another likely suspect besides Abby. I swear to you, anything you say will go only as far as it absolutely needs to go and no further. Can you help Abby out here? Can you trust me?"

It pained me to watch Ephraim's face change as I rattled on, his open smile fading to weariness as the light went out of his eyes. I squirmed under his scrutiny but managed to keep silent. Could I be trusted, or was I another opportunist trying to glean details of his misfortune? His inner conflict raged on his face.

"Why not?" he said finally. "I've been carrying this thing around for too long. It's nobody's business, but things have a way of coming out, no matter how hard you work to keep them private. Maybe now is the time. Maybe you are the person." He looked at me for a moment. "Abby Stoddard is a decent person. It's good of you to try to help her." He stood and reached to take a framed photograph down from the wall behind his desk. After blowing the dust off it, he handed it to me. "This is my daughter Amy on the day she graduated from Tufts School of Pharmacy. It was a proud day for Betsy and me. That girl is just the world to us, as sweet and fine a young woman as you would ever want to know." He stuck his head out the door to be sure Ellie and any customers were still out of earshot, then sat down again and ran a hand over his eyes.

I looked at the photograph. A sturdy, freckle-faced redhead grinned at me from beneath a black graduation cap, her new diploma held triumphantly aloft. Her eyes were clear and guileless, not those you would expect to find on a thief and a substance abuser. "So this is Amy. Actually, I've heard quite a bit about her from my daughter Emma. Did you know that they were acquainted?"

Ephraim pursed his lips and looked thoughtful. "Now that you mention it, I did know that. Went to high school together or some such, am I right?" He slapped his knee. "That's why that pretty young woman at the law barn looks so darn familiar."

I nodded. "Yes, that's Emma. She went to high school in Newington, not Wethersfield, but she and Amy knew a lot of the same kids. She told me she went to a party at your home once and was introduced to you. You have a very good memory for faces," I told him.

"Mmm, yes, it's a help in my line of work."

I sat up straighter and got to the hard part. "Emma told me something else, Ephraim. She hasn't told anyone else. In fact, she only remembered it this morning, but I think it bears on the matter at hand." As factually and non-judgmentally as I could, I laid out for him the story Emma had shared with me earlier in the day. To my relief, Ephraim seemed almost glad that I already knew about Amy's Vicodin addiction. He nodded from time to time as I spoke, confirming what Emma had suspected.

"So you know how she got hooked. That's good," he commented when I finished telling him what I knew. "But there's more to the story, much more." He paused to gather his thoughts. The phone rang at the prescription counter, and Ellie picked it up, and then poked her head around the partition.

"It's Lydia Wentworth, Ephraim, wanting to speak to you. Shall I tell her you'll call her back?"

He nodded vaguely. "Would you? I'll just be another few minutes here." She vanished again, and Ephraim picked up the story where I had left off. "Vicodin is a tricky medication. It's a very effective pain reliever, which Lord only knows Amy needed after her second knee surgery. The trouble is that it's also a mood-altering drug. It produces a euphoric feeling, and patients don't want to give it up. They begin to obsess about how they are going to get more and more of it. Pretty soon, they can't function normally without it. Even though the pain is gone, or mostly gone, the Vicodin produces an effect in them that they feel they can't live without. When the prescriptions run out, they start looking for outside sources for more pills. I've seen it happen many times, but when it got hold of our Amy…" He stopped, obviously distressed by the memory.

After a few minutes, he regained control of his voice and continued. "Amy worked part-time in the pharmacy during breaks from college. It was during spring break after the second operation that I started to suspect she was helping herself to Vicodin from the controlled substance cabinet. I noticed we were short, and I couldn't account for the discrepancy, so I questioned Ellie and Joanna, my other pharmacist about it. Joanna confessed that Amy had told her she spilled half of one of those big bottles down the sink. She didn't really believe Amy at the time, but she didn't want to tattle on my daughter to me, either, so she kept quiet and hoped I'd get wise on my own. I did, but not in the way Joanna had hoped."

At this point in his story, Ephraim went far inside himself. He sat, eyes staring at the wall beyond my shoulder, hands clasped tightly on the desk, seeming to shrivel before my eyes. "It was that harridan who confronted me," he said, his jaw clenched.

"Prudence Crane?" I asked, although I had no doubt who he meant.

"Up until then, Amy had been very discreet, kept her secret pretty well, but she got sloppy. She let Prudy see her washing pills down her throat at the diner counter one evening after she got off work, a whole handful of them. When Amy went to the restroom, Prudy took her chance and rummaged through her book bag in the counter. Found half a bottle of Vicodin and then waited for Amy to come out of the bathroom. Told her there was no way Tufts University was going to give a diploma to a junkie and probably I'd lose my license when the truth came out, as she intended to see it would. She suggested that Amy could pay for her silence on an ongoing basis, however." He shook his head in disbelief and met my eyes. "Can you believe it? She blackmailed a kid—*my* kid."

I sat for a moment, imagining how I would have felt if some predator had pulled such a thing on Emma, and my blood boiled for him. "What did Amy do then, Ephraim?"

He raised his eyebrows, clearly surprised that I had to ask. "Why, she came to her mother and me, of course, and we helped her. In many ways, that was the wake-up call she needed. We could have sent her off to a de-tox clinic, but we did some research and discovered it was possible to taper off the drug, if you have the right kind of support, and Amy did. We spent the next several months de-toxing her at home with the help of a doctor friend of ours. We tapered her off, just like they do at the private clinics. She went through bouts of diarrhea and vomiting, chills and sweats, panic attacks, and insomnia. But in the end, we won. She got off the Vicodin and stayed off it for good. So Prudy had nowhere to go with her information. Universities can do drug screens on their students, but they can't do comprehensive background checks. As long as Amy stayed clean and passed any drug screen that might come along, there was nothing Prudy could do."

"So why were you spotted giving Prudy money at the diner?"

Ephraim scowled again. "It happened after that photograph was taken, after Amy graduated. Betsy and I were so proud of our girl that day, we didn't know what to do with ourselves. She had grown so much through her experience. In fact, it helped her make a decision about the kind of work she wanted to do. Instead of coming back here to work in the store, or working for someone else, she applied for work as a compliance officer with the Federal Drug Enforcement Administration."

"But that's wonderful!" I exclaimed.

"We thought so, too—that is, until Prudence Crandall got wind of Amy's career aspirations and came to see me. It was right here in this room, in fact, that she reminded me of the extensive background checks required for that sort of work and how she planned to let the DEA know about Amy's little problem, unless I cared to make it worth her while..." His voice trailed off. "Well, you know the rest. She had us. I couldn't allow her to destroy my daughter's future." He shrugged. "So I paid up."

I sat quietly, hoping he would answer the question I didn't want to ask. After half a minute of silence, he understood what I needed to hear.

"Oh, yes. You want to know if I killed the vicious, scandal-mongering old biddy? I admit it crossed my mind. She was threatening my daughter, my whole family, and a father has instincts." He sighed heavily. "I don't know how to convince you that I'm innocent of murder. But Kate, consider this. If I'd wanted to do in Prudy, within a few yards of where you're sitting, there are a dozen substances I could have used that would never have been detected, and I have all the knowledge necessary to pull it off. I might even have done it with an overdose of Vicodin. Now, that would have been poetic justice, wouldn't it?" He smiled without humor. "So why would I choose such a crude, detectable method?" His voice was getting louder, and I worried that we might be overheard. He slammed a hand on the desk defiantly, causing me to jump. "And most importantly, why would anyone set up a nice woman like Abby Stoddard for a murder charge? She has never been anything but decent and hardworking."

I put one hand on Ephraim's arm consolingly and made a "Ssshh!" sign with the other. From the other side of the partition came the "ting" of the service bell that sat on the counter next to the cash register. Ellie must have been called away to another part of the store. Ephraim looked startled, then rose to his feet and straightened his smock.

I nodded to indicate that I understood he needed to take care of this customer, and said aloud, "Well, thank you, Mr. Marsh for giving me your advice about those side effects. I understand everything you've told me, and I'm sure there will be no more problems in the future." We both plastered smiles on our faces and left the office area as if our consultation had been strictly pharmacist-client. At the counter, holding the copy of *Field & Stream* I had seen him browsing through earlier, stood Mort Delahanty, scowling as always. Behind him, Miriam Drinkwater was holding a package of pantyhose and looking impatiently at her watch. I wondered how long they had been standing there before ringing the service bell. "Goodbye, now," I said to Ephraim and made a beeline for the door.

~ * ~

Late that afternoon, Margo and I were pursuing the theme of peaceful coexistence between men and women. I had already told her the results of my interview with Ephraim Marsh, and we were enjoying a well-deserved happy hour before heading out for the evening. We had both kicked off our shoes and propped our ankles on opposite sides of the big desk that dominated the MACK Realty office, the better to enjoy our bourbon on the rocks, served discreetly in coffee mugs. Door closed, we sipped our drinks and listened to the Law Barn empty out as Jimmy Seidel's staff, Emma among them, twittered and giggled their way into the evening.

"Everyone's always ballyhooin' about the virtues of compromise in a successful relationship, but I've always thought it was highly overrated," Margo commented. "Think about it. Dissatisfaction is the essence of compromise. Nobody gets precisely what he wants." She took another sip of her drink.

I nodded solemnly. "So what are two middle-aged adults, trying to coexist under one roof after having their own spaces for more than a decade, supposed to do?

"Personally, I vote for negotiation and accommodation."

"Do tell."

Margo warmed to her theme, or perhaps to the bourbon. I was beginning to experience a pleasant buzz myself. "In a good negotiation, everyone leaves the table feelin' like they've won—maybe not every single thing they wanted, but somethin'. It's the difference between a screamin' match and a good debate. The screamin' feels good for the moment, but it doesn't give you a shot at amelioratin' your opponent's point of view over the long haul."

"Ameliorating?" I mocked. Margo frowned and went on.

"Then there's accommodation, which comes at a difference of opinion a whole other way. You have to say, okay, doin' X is important to you, and doin' Y is just as important to me, so out of affection and consideration, we'll accommodate each other."

"I'm afraid I'm going to need an example on that one, Teach. Try not to make it too graphically sexual, please."

"I can give you two examples, Smartass, and neither one of 'em takes place between the sheets."

I smiled encouragingly.

"You're always goin' on about Armando's insistence on drinkin' one hundred percent Colombian coffee. Nothin' else will do. And I know for a fact that you have the palate of a turnip and drink that tacky half-caf stuff in the mornin'. So instead of quarrelin' about such a silly thing, why not just make two pots of coffee, his and hers? I mean, what would it take… an extra coffee filter and two extra minutes to get everybody's day off to a good start?"

I had to admit I saw her point. "Okay, two pots of coffee. What else?"

"And if you wanted to be extra accommodatin',' you could bring him a cup in bed, since you leave for work so much earlier than he does. Who knows where that might lead?" She grinned bawdily.

"See, I knew this would wind up in the bedroom." I shook my head resignedly. "What's the second example?"

Margo thought for a moment. "Space. You're both just paralyzed with fright about givin' up your own space. So why give it up entirely?"

"You mean, we should keep both houses but live in one of them most of the time? That would sort of negate the financial benefits of living together, wouldn't it?"

Margo shook her head. "No, no, no. Having space of your own doesn't have to mean a whole house, or even a separate apartment. And now that I think about it, your place is set up perfectly. You have a bedroom and an adjoinin' bath on the first floor. In fact, you hardly even go upstairs except to your office. So Armando can have his own bedroom and bathroom upstairs all to his little ol' self, and you can retreat to your downstairs suite whenever you feel the need!" she finished triumphantly.

I stared at her. "You mean, not share a bedroom? What would people think?"

Margo snorted into her glass, an unladylike habit of hers. "Now what in the world do you care what people think? If it works for you, it's nobody's damn business, Sugar."

"You know I don't give a fig for most people's opinions. I meant Emma and Joey and Mary and Strutter... you know, *my* people. Wouldn't they think that's odd?"

"No, because all of those people know you and love you both. Besides, havin' separate bedrooms and bathrooms is considered the height of elegance these days." She tipped her glass all the way up and captured the last ice cube in her mouth, then grinned wickedly. "Of course, you could always clarify the situation by doin' what a lady of my acquaintance did when visitors were clearly wonderin' about the separate bedroom thing."

"I know I'm going to regret asking this, but what did she do?"

"She hung a beautifully framed cross-stitch on the wall outside her bedroom. It read, 'We Do It Here'." She dissolved into giggles.

I couldn't help laughing. "Couldn't you just see Philpott's face at my holiday open house?" Edna Philpott was my neighbor two doors down, a prim, self-righteous type who had appointed herself chief enforcer of the rules in my condominium community. Most of us delighted in torturing her by side-stepping minor regulations whenever we thought we could get away with it.

The thought of Edna's reaction, coupled with the bourbon we had consumed, kept us whooping. As I locked the office door, I noticed that Millie Haines' light was still on and attempted unsuccessfully to shush Margo. Millie spent her days on the go and caught up on her paperwork in the evening. The best we could do was to muffle our snorts and chortles as we made our way through the lobby. Emma's day had apparently also ended, as no light was visible when I stuck my head into the loft stairwell, so we let ourselves out the front door and locked it behind us. We wiped our eyes on a shared tissue and bid each other goodnight after agreeing on a time to meet at the Wheeler house the next morning. It promised to be an interesting day, but also one that involved a lot of work.

After an early dinner with Manny at Costa del Sol, I let myself into the condo and fed the cats, then drew my customary bubble bath. It was a peaceful way to end the day, and I had a lot to think about. When the water cooled, I levered myself out of the tub and went through my bedtime ritual of creams and potions before heading for my bed, where Jasmine and Simon already lay neatly curled to one side. It had taken years of training to make them understand that I was entitled to spread out into the middle of the mattress, but cats were expected to fit along the perimeter. When Armando spent the night, they really took issue, especially Jasmine, who considered him her personal heat source.

The crossword puzzle I held propped before me was ignored as I continued to turn over my conversation with Ephraim Marsh in my mind. On the plus side, I was convinced that he had nothing to do with Prudy's death. On the negative side, that eliminated all of the suspects Abby had asked me to question. Unless she had thought of someone else, or we found Harriett Wheeler's diaries the next day, I was out of ideas on where else to look for Prudy's murderer. I wondered if the police were having any better luck.

It was only then that I realized that Margo hadn't said a word about her evening with John Harkness, and I had forgotten to tell her about my surprising discovery in the reading room that morning. Oh, well, I thought drowsily as the puzzle slipped to the floor, and I reached to switch off my bedside table lamp, we'll have a lot to talk about tomorrow.

About that, I turned out to be right. Oh, boy, was I.

Eight

At 10:30 sharp, I drove up in front of Will and Janet Copeland's house on Wolcott Hill Road, which stood next to the old Wheeler residence. Wolcott Hill was an interesting stretch of road to a realtor, and probably to anyone else who had occasion to view its entire length. It extended south from the Hartford border to its terminus at Prospect Street, which fairly accurately bisected Wethersfield from east to west. One of the main thoroughfares in the older part of town, it had evolved over the years into a pleasing microcosm of the evolution of the town itself. Victorians, such as the Wheeler house, sat next to post-World War II frame residences, such as the Copeland's, which in turn enjoyed a '60s bungalow as its neighbor on the other side.

The pleasant jumble of building periods and styles was knit together by well-tended lawns and gardens of every shape and size, which spilled over with spider mums, kale, ornamental cabbages, and asters. Their vivid colors were set off by backdrops of thistle and decorative grasses. In this part of town, driveways were edged, and even the foundation plantings were weeded regularly. It all looked perfectly lovely, hardly what one would expect of a murder scene. But then, it wasn't a murder scene, as far as we knew. It was merely the former home of a murder victim.

I enjoyed the morning, as I waited for Margo to join me, knowing that a hard frost or two would put an end to the blooms, for the most part. Many of the perennials in the borders had already been cut back severely and mulched for the winter, and although the chrysanthemums made a brave display, they weren't nearly as hardy as most people thought. It wouldn't be long before we were compelled to settle into the drabness of November, to be followed by the white winter. Each season had a charm of its own, to be sure, but autumn was my favorite. At least it had been, until this whole business with Prudy had cast suspicion on friends, colleagues, and even my own daughter.

Impatiently, I checked my watch again. The sooner we found those diaries, the better, so where in blazes was Margo?

Right on cue, Margo slid the BMW in behind me at the curb and climbed out, yawning widely. She carried a cardboard tray with two super-sized Dunkin Donuts coffees in it. Though dressed casually, for her, in denim capris and a navy big shirt with a white tank top underneath, she was as immaculately groomed as always. I wondered yet again how she always managed to look pulled together. My own jeans pouched badly at the knees, and I had barely taken the time to swipe on lipstick and mascara.

"Sorry I was late, Sugar, but I had to drop Rhett off at his pen behind the office and pick us up some caffeine, if I'm goin' to be of any use at all today."

She yawned again, and I noticed the dark smudges beneath her eyes.

"Hot date, huh?" I said too casually as I reached for a coffee, and she clammed up instantly. Margo would talk when Margo was good and ready. I got the message and veered into a new subject. "Where do we begin? I've been sitting here for several minutes, but Janet and Will don't seem interested in joining us."

"Uh uh, no way," Margo said, taking a pull on her coffee. "The quicker those folks can unload this property, the happier they'll be, and in the meantime, it'll be just us. Where's Emma?"

"She'll be along later. After the week she's had, I told her she could sleep in."

Margo nodded. "Okay, then, let's do this." She handed me the tray and produced the set of large, old-fashioned keys we had seen earlier. "As soon as I figure out which one of these opens the front door, I'll put it in a lockbox. I've got one in the car."

A lockbox was a device used by virtually all realtors to avoid having to keep track of hundreds of individual house keys for their listings. The key to each listing was placed in a small, box that hung from the knob on the front door. All of the lockboxes could be opened with a single key, which the realtor carried.

The gray house sat quietly behind its forest green shutters, patiently awaiting its fate as it had for so many years. I was humbled, as I always was in the presence of old trees and old buildings, by the knowledge of how much they had witnessed and endured. This one had been built in 1925, so it had survived the Great Depression and World War II in addition to the calamitous world events that had occurred in my time, plus a couple of dozen more winters and hurricanes. Yet here it sat with its rocking-chair porch and windowed sunroom, dozing serenely in the late-season sunshine, oblivious to the fact that one of its occupants had been brutally murdered.

Inside, we fumbled for a wall switch in the dim interior. I located one to the right of the door and switched on the elegant, crystal-faceted ceiling fixture that graced the modest foyer. Janet and Will had obviously done a lot of work on the first floor. Without needing to discuss it, we could see that the house would show very well—and quickly, too. Properties for sale in Wethersfield were few and far between in this market. Original hardwood floors and moldings led gracefully from a fireplaced sitting room to a formal dining room, eat-in kitchen, the sunroom, and a tiled bath. The rooms were smallish but well-proportioned, and light spilled in from the windows on all sides. I knew from the listing that the house boasted a full basement, something many others of its era did not have. I sincerely hoped it would not be necessary to search there for Harriett Wheeler's diaries, however.

Leaving our belongings in the kitchen, we finished our tour of the first level and climbed slowly up the wide stairs to what had been Prudy Crane's living quarters. A heavy door at the top of the staircase separated the apartment from the lower part of the house, and once again, Margo negotiated the key chain successfully. The cleaning crew had removed the yellow crime scene tape, but I was apprehensive as she eased open the door. Almost fearfully, I peered over her shoulder.

Instead of the rabbit warren of tiny rooms I had expected on the second story of this old structure, we stepped into a large, sunny studio apartment. Structurally, the space was very interesting since it had obviously been created by knocking down several interior walls. The result was one open room, flooded with light from the large windows on the back wall. The plainness of the room was alleviated by its buttercup yellow walls and a number of appealing nooks and niches, in which hung some beautifully framed botanical prints. A large, decorative column rose from the floor in the center of the room, apparently replacing a weight-bearing wall of years past.

A doorway to our right led into a tiny, but nicely equipped, galley kitchen and an equally well-appointed bathroom. The focal point of the main room was a small, gas fireplace on the left wall. It boasted a hand-carved mantelpiece and was flanked by built-in bookcases, which held hundreds of hardcover novels. Many were expensively bound in leather, and most of them seemed to be mysteries. Agatha Christie and Ngaio Marsh jostled for space with Joan Hess and Lisa Scottoline, Josephine Tey and P.D. James. Lillian Braun's *The Cat Who* titles shared a shelf with Nancy Atherton's *Aunt Dimity* series.

A slipcovered club chair and ottoman sat before the fireplace along with a drop-leaf table, which held a shaded lamp and one tidy coaster. The absence of a television confirmed that reading was Prudy's preferred recreational activity—that is, when she wasn't out collecting payments from her blackmail victims. The rest of the room was devoted to a comfy-looking brass bedstead piled high with comforter and pillows, a night table, and an old-fashioned armoire.

"Well, let's get to it," Margo sighed. "This is pretty much our only opportunity to find those danged diaries, and we can't make a mess doin' it. We have to show this place tomorrow, remember."

"Mmm," I agreed looking for a logical place to start. "What do you think these diaries might look like?"

Margo thought about it. "When I was a kid, I kept a diary one year. My mama gave it to me for Christmas—you know, one of those little books with a leather strap and a lock that could be picked by anybody with a paper clip. It was months before I realized my little sister was readin' it to her friends and gigglin' on the phone every night."

I couldn't help chuckling myself. "So you think they look something like that?"

"Hell, no. Harriett wrote a bunch of G-rated romance novels back in the '50s and '60s, right?"

I nodded.

"So I'm thinking somethin' girly with one of those satin ribbon thingies attached at the top to mark her place. Of course, I'm just speculatin' here."

"Well, it's as good a theory as any. Tell you what. I'll tackle the kitchen and bathroom, and you start out here, and we can share anything that looks interesting. If we don't find them up here, we'll go down to the first floor and look, but I'm hoping we'll get lucky up here."

"Sounds like a plan to me." I left her opening the door to the armoire and trudged into the kitchen to tackle the cupboards. A small window cheered the utilitarian space. Fortunately, Prudy seemed to eat most of her meals at the diner, limiting her use of the kitchen to making cups of tea and indulging a taste for macaroons. Except for these items, a canister of granulated sugar, a half-empty bottle of scotch, and half a dozen cans of soup, her cupboards were bare. The pickings were equally slim in her compact refrigerator, which held half a pint of spoiled half-and-half, two desiccated lemons, a few eggs, and some flat soda water, which I assumed went with the scotch.

An hour later, as I was replacing the drawer beneath the oven, which I had conscientiously removed to search behind, I was out of ideas. I had pulled the refrigerator out of its niche, disassembled and looked beneath the dishwasher, tapped all of the walls and cupboards in kitchen and bath for hollow spots, and emptied every container of food and cleanser, just in case a key had been concealed within one of them. I had filled a big trash bag, from Prudy's stash under the sink, and dragged it disconsolately into the living room to check on Margo's progress. I found her flat on her back underneath the brass bed, poking the underside of the mattress.

"Well, I'm out of places to look," I announced. "Any luck in here?"

"Not unless you want to start pulling off the crown molding," Margo sighed. "Help me out from under this thing."

I grabbed her ankles and yanked, and she slid smoothly across the hardwood.

"If I have a splinter in my backside, I'll know who to blame," she complained and clambered to her feet, dusting off the seat of her pants. "Huh, that Grace does a great job. There aren't too many places where you can crawl around on the floor under the bed and come up clean."

"She's one in a million," I agreed. "So were you kidding about the crown molding?"

"I think so." Margo stood with her hands on her shapely hips as she surveyed the tops of the walls. Even tired and slightly grubby, she looked gorgeous. I wondered again about her relationship with John Harkness, but I knew better than to ask. "You've got to figure there were a bunch of volumes, and that molding just wouldn't conceal a big enough hidey hole. Mrs. Wheeler kept a diary all of her life, Mavis said."

"Yes, but maybe Prudy only kept the juicy ones. I

mean, how many scandals could a little New England town generate in Harriett Wheeler's lifetime? For all we know, her own daughter's situation might be the only scandal she wrote about... if she even wrote about that. There might have been only one volume worth stealing, for Prudy's purposes."

"Good point. Still, I've been over everything in this room with a fine-toothed comb—floors, walls, furniture. Nothing. So much as I hate to say it, I guess we'd better suck it up and head downstairs, Sugar."

Unenthusiastically, I agreed, and together we bumped the bag of trash down the stairs to the first floor. My stomach had been growling for some time, and the stale macaroon I had scarfed from Prudy's larder hadn't done much to ward off hunger. I was cheered to see Emma heading up the front walk with what I hoped was lunch in a large paper sack.

Margo was apparently as hungry as I was. "Hey," was all Emma had time to say before we relieved her of her burden and fell upon the bagel sandwiches within. While Margo and I munched, Emma ran lithely up the stairs to check out Prudy's apartment. When she returned, we all trooped out to the back porch to sit in the sun for a few minutes while we filled Emma in on our progress, or lack of it.

Refreshed, and with young muscles to help us, we returned to the search. Emma tackled the big kitchen downstairs, while I investigated the sitting and dining rooms. Margo snooped thoroughly around the sunroom and bathroom. With the exception of the mailman, who startled us in mid-afternoon when he saw the lights on inside and rang the doorbell to see if the house had new occupants, we were undisturbed. By five o'clock, as the sunlight faded, we had exhausted every possibility we could think of and were ready to call it quits. Two more trash bags filled with construction debris and the remains of our lunch joined the first one on the rocking chair porch, and we formed a discouraged little posse on the stairs.

"So now what?" Emma asked the obvious. "The basement?"

"At night, in the dark? I don't think so," I demurred, and Margo shuddered.

"I don't see any other choice," Emma insisted.

I put my head in my hands and tried to think. We knew Prudy was getting her information from a number of sources. She was an inveterate snoop, and her eyes and ears were always open for an opportunity to put the squeeze on another victim. When Janet and Will were clearing out Harriett Wheelers books, and she saw those boxes filled with personal papers, she would have found them irresistible. I had no doubt that she would have pounced on them. I just didn't know whether Harriett's diaries were in them. For all we knew, Harriett burned them or buried them long before she died in order to carry Mavis' secret to her grave. But if she had done that, how had Prudy discovered the truth? I groaned in frustration, and Emma rubbed my back sympathetically.

"Okay, that's enough for one day," Margo announced. "Shoo, shoo now!" She jumped to her feet and waved her hands at us. "Go get yourselves some dinner. Take the trash to the Law Barn dumpster on the way, and I'll lock up here."

"You're not coming with us?" I protested. "We need to figure out a game plan for tomorrow."

"Honey, I've held enough open houses in the past year to dance through this one backwards and in high heels just like Adele Astaire, so don't you fret. For your information, I'm seeing John tonight—yes, again," she said as Emma's mouth opened, "and you can both mind your own business." Emma's mouth clacked shut. "I'll just make one more run through the house to make sure everythin's tidy, and then I'll be on my way. Go on now!"

Emma and I exchanged looks and got obediently to our feet. We knew when we were licked.

Twenty minutes later, we perched on bar stools at On the Border and sipped cold Coronas while we racked our brains. Exploring the basement of that spooky Victorian, even with company, appealed to me not at all. I put the topic aside for the moment. "Millie Haines is an interesting character," I said and recounted my conversation of the previous day in the lobby. "She's a funny mix of middle-aged professional and Valley Girl, all real estate jargon one minute and girlish slang the next. I didn't quite know what to make of her, but she seemed to think quite a lot of you," I mused.

"I know what you mean. She seems competent enough,

but all that 'Hey there!' and 'Way cool!' stuff seems odd coming from a woman of her age," Emma agreed.

"The thing is, she reminds me of someone. That sweet face and big brown eyes with the loooong lashes. Sort of reminds me of —" I stopped short and looked at Emma.

"Elsie the Cow!" we both finished my thought.

"Oh my god, Emma, she's the spitting image of Mavis Griswold. She could *be* Mavis Griswold twenty years ago. It's the Jersey shag haircut that threw me off, and the heavy eye make-up. Otherwise, I would have seen it right away." In my excitement, I took too big a swallow and choked. Emma thumped me between the shoulder blades, and the bartender looked our way with concern. When I could stop wiping my eyes, I mopped my nose with a napkin.

"Easy, there, Big Girl," Emma admonished. "Slow down, or you'll have a stroke. Do you really think," she looked cautiously over both shoulders and lowered her voice, "that Millie could be Mavis' long-lost daughter?"

"She's the right age. She told me herself she's forty-five, and Mavis' and Henry's daughter was born forty-five years ago. She's from California, which is where Mavis went to have the baby and gave her up for adoption. And she looks so much like Mavis, it's scary. How much more convincing do you need?" I was practically bouncing up and down with excitement.

"More than that," Emma said with conviction, "and anyway, it's not a matter of convincing me. We just need to find out if it's true, because if it is, that gives Millie

Haines a motive for murdering Prudy Crane, and we could really use another suspect right about now."

Our burgers arrived, and we munched thoughtfully, washing down big bites with the Coronas. Emma wolfed down her fries and reached for mine, and I slapped her hand away automatically. "Not a chance. Listen, there's got to be a fairly easy way to find out who Millie Haines really is."

"Maybe she's really Millie Haines," Emma pointed out reasonably enough. "Even if she is Mavis' daughter, she was adopted, remember? She could have any name at all."

"True. We need some basic information in order to research her background, like previous addresses, places of employment, that sort of thing. There might be something in her office." I kept my eyes on my burger as Emma thought that over.

"Are you actually suggesting that we—"

"Yes."

"Tonight? I thought you had plans with Manny."

"He won't mind if I'm a little late, so why not do it? It's Saturday, and presumably, even mortgage brokers take Saturday night off. We'll never have a better opportunity. Besides, we have to take the trash to the Law Barn dumpster anyway. We could just check things out, poke around a little, see what we can see."

"Welcome to the Kate Lawrence cliché festival," Emma said and drained the last of her beer. She put her glass down with a thump and swiped a napkin over her mouth. "Check, please," she said to the bartender.

"But I'm not through yet!" I protested.

"You are if you want my help. I've been stuck in that loft all week, and I have a life, too, you know. I have no intention of spending the whole night skulking around Millie Haines' office. It's probably locked anyway. So show me your money, Sherlock, and let's hit the road."

~ * ~

As we had hoped, except for the shaded lamp that burned softly on Jenny's desk, the Law Barn was dark when we let ourselves in the front door. We had traveled there separately and driven as close to the building as we could, tucking both cars into the overhanging shrubbery next to the driveway. I had been there at night only occasionally, and frankly, I was glad of Emma's company this time. The old building was full of cracks that caught the wind, not to mention Emma's friends, the mice, and the combined rustlings and creaks could be really creepy.

Cautiously, we locked the door behind ourselves to prevent being surprised by any conscientious colleagues who decided to put in a few hours over the weekend, but at month's end, that was extremely unlikely anyway. As we started through the empty lobby, I remembered that I hadn't yet told Emma and Margo about the listening tube in the reading room. "Wait a minute! You have got to see this," I told her and led the way through the coatroom.

As I expected, Emma was enchanted by my discovery and insisted on taking advantage of our opportunity to locate the other end of the conduit. I remained in the reading room and recited the lyrics of Tom Lehrer's deliciously satirical song, "Oedipus Rex," into my end of the tube while Emma scurried into the lobby to hear what she could hear. "There once was a man named Oedipus Rex. You may have heard about his odd complex. His name appears in Freud's index 'cause he... loved his mother. The neighbors used to say quite a bit that as a monarch, he was most unfit. Still and all, they had to admit that he... loved his mother!"

I distinctly heard Emma's groan. "Okay, stop, stop!" I stopped and listened as she tapped her way along the wall behind Jenny's desk.

"I can hear you, but I can't tell where you are yet."

Then I heard a strange, scraping sound. "What are you doing now?"

"Hellooooo, 'Cita!" Emma's merry voice floated into the reading room loudly enough to make me jump. "I'm speaking to you from directly behind Mr. Watercolors' awful portrait. He really was a piece of work, wasn't he?"

I ran out of the reading room to join her. It was true. By tilting the gilt-framed portrait slightly, Emma had revealed the other end of the conduit. It wasn't covered. The edge of the frame held the bulk of the portrait sufficiently far away from its mouth to allow ambient sound to enter easily. No wonder I had been able to hear Jenny on the phone. It was good to have that little mystery solved, at least. Now we had to get serious about our mission before somebody walked in and caught us.

As it happened, Millie had left her office door not only unlocked but open, which didn't strike me as a good idea until we attempted to pull open the drawers of her desk and file cabinet. All were securely locked. Although the trees and hedge that ran along a chain link fence at the back of the property shielded us from the direct view of neighbors across the back alley, I felt exposed standing in the lighted office in front of Millie's unshaded window, which had been left open an inch to air out for the weekend. I just wanted to find whatever basic information about Millie there was to be found and then beat it for home, where Armando was waiting for me. Equally eager to meet her own friends, Emma looked as frustrated as I felt. We both looked around the room bleakly.

"If she has any secrets, she knows how to keep them," I said, "much like Harriett Wheeler. Maybe it's a family trait," I speculated, bitter from a day's unproductive sleuthing. I was tired and grubby and wanted nothing so much as a hot bath and a long snuggle with my fella. "Any ideas?"

Emma was staring fixedly at Millie's desk, and I followed her gaze. There in plain sight was an old-fashioned Rolodex, dog-eared cards spewing out from every angle. "Can you believe it?" She touched it with awe. "The woman is a dinosaur! Nobody keeps their contacts on cards these days. Do you suppose...?"

I snatched it up eagerly and headed for the anteroom. "Never mind the chitchat. Fire up the copy machine, and let's get this done."

We worked quickly as a team, carefully removing the cards from the Rolodex and laying them out on the glass of the copy machine. We used the largest paper it held, eleven by seventeen inches, so we could cover a lot of ground quickly. In less than twenty minutes, we had successfully copied and reassembled the spinning file, artfully replacing all the inserted scraps of paper as well. Emma punched off the machine, and we scuttled back to Millie's office. I replaced the Rolodex on her desk and took a final look around to make sure we had covered our tracks. And then we heard it—the sound of someone else unlocking the front door.

Horrified, I grabbed for the copies we'd made and knocked a mug full of pens and pencils all over the floor. With no time to pick things up, Emma hit the light switch, I stuffed the copies into my handbag, and we groped our way out of Millie's office. We'd never make it to the reading room, so we headed for the back door, feeling our way along the wall. Luckily, whoever was trying to come in was evidently having trouble getting the key to work, so we had time to pull open the back door and ease out onto the porch.

Pulling the back door shut as quietly as I could, I felt my way down the porch stairs behind Emma and flattened myself next to her against the building. Suddenly, light spilled from Millie's window over our heads. "What the—? Oh, it must have been that damned dog," we heard her say, then the clinks and clunks of writing implements being collected and dropped back into the mug. We waited, hardly daring to breathe. *If she spotted us, what on earth could we say to her?* One minute passed, then two, as Millie apparently went about her business, opening and closing desk drawers and her file cabinet. As we tried to summon the nerve to tiptoe out to the back alley, scrabbling could be heard in the leaves near the trash cans, which stood near a chain link fence. Prickles of alarm ran down my spine. I grabbed Emma's arm and put my mouth close to her ear. "Friend of yours, or rodent unknown?"

She shushed me and peered into the darkness. "It's probably Jake, scrounging a snack," she whispered, and to my horror, she started toward the trash cans. I'm an animal lover, too, but confronting an unknown animal in the dark felt very risky. Connecticut had had a rabies outbreak among its raccoons and other critters not too many years ago, which is why even housecats have to be inoculated every three years now. Emma fumbled in her jeans and came up with her car keys, which jingled alarmingly to my overstretched nerves. On one hand, I didn't want Millie to get the wind up. If we could hear her moving around inside, she could probably hear us, too. On the other, some noise might encourage whatever was raiding the trash cans to call it a night. Emma's keychain had a pen light attached, which she switched on and aimed toward the trash cans, despite my waving at her frantically to cease and desist.

"Ohhh, it's Fat Squirrel!" she whispered far too loudly for my comfort. "He's stuck in the fence." She knelt down in the gravel.

"Emma, don't go near him, for god's sake, he might be rabid!" I blurted and threw caution to the wind. I reached her side in three running steps and attempted to pull her to her feet. Then I saw the sad little scene that she had already assessed. It was indeed Fat Squirrel. His head and most of his torso were on the far side of the chain link fence, but his hindquarters were solidly stuck on our side, his rear paws twisted in the remains of a plastic bag. How long he had been trapped there, it was hard to guess. Since squirrels retire at dusk, it was safe to say he'd been stuck for at least several hours, and he panted with exhaustion. It was only a matter of time before Jake found him on night patrol and made a late snack of him. Emma and I looked at each other.

"We can't just leave him here," Emma pleaded.

My head said yes, we could, but my heart agreed with her. The poor little guy looked done in as his sides heaved in the small pool of light. "Okay, okay. He can't bite us with his head stuck on the other side of the fence. I've got some nail scissors in here somewhere. We'll cut the bag off his back feet, and he can go on his way." I rummaged in the recesses of my handbag, and Emma aimed her light inside to help.

Just then, the floodlights over the back porch came on, fully illuminating the small yard, and Millie Haines stepped cautiously out of the door holding her cell phone. She shielded her eyes with her free hand and peered toward us. "Who's out there?" she quavered. "Whoever you are, you should know that I've already called the police, and they're on their way."

I groaned. "Perfect!" I snapped at Emma. "Now we get

to explain ourselves to Millie *and* to the Wethersfield police." I turned toward the porch and waved feebly at Millie. "It's Kate and Emma, Millie. We're trying to get a squirrel unstuck from the chain link fence." It sounded pretty strange, even to me, but Millie smiled with evident relief at the sound of my voice and bounded down the steps.

"Well, hey, you guys! What's going on? Can I help?" She seemed totally unfazed by our presence in the back yard of the law barn after dark on a Saturday and as eager as a puppy to be included in whatever was going on.

Emma snatched my handbag and rummaged around in the bottom. "Found 'em!" she announced triumphantly, holding my nail scissors aloft. "Now stand back a few feet, and let me get this thing off him." She knelt to her task, and I held the pen light over her head.

Millie watched over my shoulder. "Eeeuuww! It's all hairy and gross looking. Are you sure it's a squirrel? Don't squirrels bite?"

The sound of a police siren wailed in the distance. "Only if they're rabid, and we're pretty sure this one isn't," I snapped less than reassuringly. Millie took a step backwards. The police siren got louder as the patrol car neared the Law Barn. A couple of other porch lights went on in the neighborhood. "The police seem to be here. Maybe you should go tell them it was a false alarm while we finish up here."

"Well, okay, if you think I should," Millie responded eagerly, backing farther away. She broke into a trot and headed back inside.

"There!" Emma exclaimed as the final shred of plastic fell away from the squirrel's hind legs. For half a second, he remained frozen, unable to believe that he was free at last. Then with one final heave, he was through the fence and gone, the scraps of plastic Emma held the only evidence that he had ever been there. "You're welcome!" Emma called after him, but her sarcasm was probably lost on F.S.

"Okay, great," I tried to get her head back to our present situation. "Now quick, what are we going to tell these cops?"

But it was too late to collaborate on a story. Apparently, Millie had not been successful in calling off the emergency visit, because the back door opened once again, and two burly young officers tromped down the steps. I was pleased to see that the one who was brandishing a large torch was Rick Fletcher. Maybe there was hope for us yet. Cautiously, Rick moved his torch from me to Emma and back again. Millie, coward that she was, hung back from the scene.

"Evening, Emma, Miz Lawrence," he said dryly and switched off his light. I felt as guilty and as ridiculous as I'm sure I looked, huddled next to my daughter in the glare of the floodlights. If possible, Emma looked even less plausible. She held my handbag in one hand and her car keys in the other, a few scraps of torn plastic peeking from her fist. There was no car in sight and nowhere to park one.

"Hey, Rick," said Emma. "We were rescuing a squirrel that got stuck in the fence."

"Uh-huh," Rick responded with a straight face. I was willing to bet he was a first rate poker player. "Officer Chapman here and I are responding to a 911 call made by Miz Haines a few minutes ago. She told the dispatcher that there were strange noises coming from the rear of the Law Barn and asked us to investigate, believing that the property might be the target of vandals."

Officer Chapman was a sturdy towhead who looked enough like Rick to be his brother. Though he wasn't very tall and looked like a youngster to me, he was probably around thirty and packed enough muscle beneath his uniform shirt to inspire respect. He nodded briefly in agreement. "When we arrived, Miz Haines met us at the front door and explained that she had discovered the source of the noises to be a…" he consulted a small notepad, "…rodent of some sort."

Millie smiled and nodded helpfully. "That's right. Kate and Emma said it was a squirrel, but when I saw it, it looked much bigger, and hairy, like maybe a—"

"It was a squirrel," Emma repeated, "one I know personally. He had his back feet caught in a plastic bag, because he'd been raiding our trashcans, even though I put peanuts out for him today, so he really shouldn't have, and he got stuck halfway through the chain link, and I couldn't just leave him here for Jake to eat, so I cut the plastic off, and he ran away."

I encouraged her to stop blathering with a hard pinch.

She winced and held up the pieces of plastic and my nail scissors.

Rick stared at her for a two-count, and then turned to Chapman. "Ron, I don't think we have anything ongoing here. Mind calling it in?"

"No problem," said Chapman. He flipped his notebook shut and trudged around the corner of the Law Barn back to the patrol car that was presumably parked out front.

Millie tittered self-consciously. "Well, if there's nothing else you need from me, Officer…" Clearly, she wanted to make her escape, and Rick let her off the hook.

"If we need any information for our report, we know where to find you, ma'am. You have a good evening now."

"Okay, if you're sure. Bye Kate, Emma!" And she fled back into the building.

Rick returned his attention to Emma and me.

"Ma'am?" Emma twitted him. "Nice touch."

Rick didn't take the bait. "Maybe you'd like to tell me what the two of you were doing prowling around out here in the dark on a Saturday evening?"

Judging from the number of porch lights that now peppered the dark, I imagined that the neighbors would like to know that, too. "I stopped by to pick up… some files," I said.

"…my jacket," Emma ended simultaneously.

We glared at each other, and Rick glared at both of us.

"And you keep your files in the back yard?"

I looked at Emma, and she deferred to me with an *after*

you gesture. God only knew where the lie came from, but it rolled right off the tip of my tongue. "We spent the afternoon with my partner, Margo Farnsworth, getting the old Wheeler property ready for an open house tomorrow afternoon. Margo's dog Rhett spent the afternoon here in his pen, and Margo forgot to collect his favorite chew toy when she picked him up. She knew I had to swing by here to collect some files," I shot a warning glance at Emma, "and asked me to pick it up. If Rhett doesn't have his favorite toy, he'll drive us crazy tomorrow. You know how dogs are." I tried my most winning smile.

"So where's the toy?" Rick wanted to know.

"Yeah, where's the toy?" Emma chimed in viciously, but I was up to the challenge. Because I'd put Rhett into his pen yesterday, I knew which toys stayed there. "Gee, thanks for reminding me! In all the confusion about the squirrel, I forgot all about it. It's a rubber bone that squeaks. Be a dear and get it for us, would you, Rick?"

But Rick was not to be deflected so easily. "Be glad to in a minute. Would you be good enough to give me Miz Farnsworth's phone number? I'll need to have her corroborate your story. It's just routine for the report." He smiled blandly, his pencil poised above his notebook. *Gotcha.*

Looking as if she were watching a tennis match, Emma swiveled her attention back to me and raised an eyebrow.

Oh, no, you don't, I smiled back at Rick. Did this kid really think he could outmaneuver a woman who had survived raising two teenagers? "Her cell phone number is

209-1515, but I doubt that you'll be able to reach her right now. I believe she's at dinner with Lieutenant Harkness again this evening, isn't she, Em?"

Emma turned to Rick with interest. He didn't change expression, but he finished writing and snapped the notebook shut. "I'll try her later then." He tromped off to the dog pen to collect Rhett's squeaky toy.

Check and mate.

~ * ~

I arrived home more than two hours later than I had told Manny I'd be there, and he was nowhere to be seen. All that was waiting for me in my totally dark house were two hungry, huffy cats. I imagined that Manny was in much the same condition, since I had turned off my cell phone during dinner and never turned it back on again. I've tried time and again to explain that I consider cell phones major contributors to noise pollution, not to mention hellishly dangerous while driving. I carry mine for emergencies only, but he insists on getting his feelings hurt when I don't answer it.

At the moment, I was too weary to worry about it. Manny was a big boy. He'd get over it. I did feel bad about the cats missing their dinner, though, and hurried to make amends. Jasmine accepted a scratch and a bowl of her favorite chicken and herring, served on the pass-through between the kitchen and dining room, and Simon wove annoyingly between my ankles as I struggled to place his dish of wet food sprinkled liberally with crunchies next to his water bowl.

That done, I headed for the bathtub but checked the house phone for messages first. Sure enough, the light was blinking, and the indicator showed two messages had been left. I felt sure that at least one of them was a blistering Latino rant. Well, Manny might be mad as hell, but at least he was speaking to me. I braced myself and pressed "Play."

"Hope you're having a lovely evenin' with that good lookin' man of yours, Sugar, but I simply could not wait to tell you the news. I found the diaries, can you believe it? I got to thinking about where I'd hide somethin' in that little place of Prudy's, if I had to, and I kept comin' back to the idea of hidin' in plain sight. You know, if you want to hide a file folder, you stick it in a drawer with a hundred other file folders and label it somethin' totally unrelated to what's really in there. So where would I hide a book? Why, in a big bunch of other books, naturally! And I ran back up the stairs to Prudy's apartment and started openin' the covers of all those mystery novels on her bookshelves, and voila! You know, my mama was so right, you should never judge a book by its cover. The one I'm holdin' in my hand right this minute might say Agatha Christie on the outside, but it is pure Harriett Wheeler on the inside!"

I shook my head in disgust. *Didn't that just figure?* We had wasted an entire day looking for something that wasn't even hidden. Well, at least we hadn't compounded our error by spending the evening poking around in that creepy basement. Sighing, I pushed "play" to hear my second message.

"It's Abby, Kate. I'm so sorry to have to intrude on your evening, but I just don't know where else to turn. I've been arrested for the murder of Prudy Crane."

My heart skipped at least one beat, and I clutched the phone to my ear. *Poor Abby!*

"I need your help once again."

Not that I've been much help so far, I thought, chagrined at this new development.

"Because I'm the sole caretaker for my mother, and I have a business in town and all, they're willing to release me if I can post bail. It's five hundred thousand dollars. I'll have to put up the diner and my house as collateral. Please, Kate…" Abby paused again to try to pull herself together, "…Do what you can to find a bail bondsman. I tried your cell phone, but you didn't answer there either. My neighbor is in the house with Mom, but I can't impose on her much longer. I really need your help. I don't know how much longer I can keep silent."

Nine

On Sunday morning, I went to meet Margo for late breakfast at the Town Line Diner, so named because it was located in a shopping plaza on the line between Wethersfield and Rocky Hill. Manny and I often lingered over a big diner breakfast at the counter most Sunday mornings, served ably and cheerfully by Janice or Angie or Sherri, because the coffee was good enough to please even a particular Colombian.

This morning, I particularly enjoyed the familiar bustle and chatter as I followed the hostess to a booth in the large back room. I wasn't in a good mood. It had taken me half the night to arrange for Abby's bail and get her released. Her bond had been set by the arraigning judge at $500,000, as she had told me, and she had to put up her house and the diner as collateral. If this thing went wrong, Abby would lose everything and spend many years in prison. Who would look after her ailing mother then?

While driving Abby back to her house, I attempted to bolster her spirits with an abbreviated account of my activities since she and I had first talked. It was hard to gauge her frame of mind. She sat stiffly in the seat beside me, hands gripping each other, staring straight before her. She had aged ten years in the last week. By the time I got her home to her mother, it was well after 2 a.m.

In addition to being sleep deprived and worried sick that Emma's name would soon be given to the police as an alternative suspect, I was tired of avoiding Ephraim Marsh and Mavis Griswold, both of whom had good reason to be full of anxious questions. I was tired of the no-smoking ban protestors who continued to pace and shout and clutter the sidewalks. And I was tired of quarreling with Manny, who was still pouting about last night. We had plans to take his *Tia* Estella to a late afternoon performance at Hartford Stage for her birthday, and I wasn't looking forward to hearing more from him on the subject of silly women who have, but refuse to use, cell phones.

Emma had been unavailable by phone since we had separated the previous evening, so I had no idea what she was up to, and Joey was in town, looking for a home-cooked dinner, which I would be unable to provide because I'd be out with my pissed-off man and his auntie. At the moment, Joey was sleeping in my guestroom, so I left him a note about my having breakfast with Margo at the diner.

In the meantime, there was the open house to get through, as well as Harriett Wheeler's diaries. Arriving only a moment behind me, Margo lugged them to the diner in an elegant leather tote, which she deposited beneath our table. "Whew! These things are heavy. Where's the coffee?" An obliging waiter appeared with a filled cup, and she busied herself with a packet of sweetener. "What's wrong, Sugar? You're wearin' a mighty long face for a Sunday mornin'."

I enumerated the events of the previous evening, finishing up with, "...And on top of everything else, Manny and I aren't speaking."

She smiled sympathetically. "Nothin' worse than gettin' into it with your honey bun to start a day off badly," she agreed.

I sipped my coffee. "That doesn't seem to be a problem for you these days," I noted recklessly. "Ready to talk about the big romance yet, or must I really keep pretending not to have noticed that you and John Harkness have become an item?"

Margo regarded me levelly over the rim of her cup. After assessing me for a moment, she decided not to pick a fight. "Well, since you ask." She put down her cup. "The situation is this. Yes, John and I are seein' quite a lot of each other. He is an absolutely darlin' man, and I enjoy his company tremendously. And no, we are not discussin' Prudy Crane's murder investigation. That topic is completely off limits. Except for that first time I went to the police station, we do not ask each other about it, and we do not tell each other about it. Is that what you wanted to know?"

"Basically, thanks. Sorry I'm in such a foul temper. Cheer me up with some juicy details, since I'm getting my romance vicariously these days." I grinned apologetically, and Margo grinned back. Peace restored, we ordered bodacious omelets and girl-talked all the way through them and two more cups of coffee before reluctantly turning our attention to the tote bag at our feet.

"How many diaries are there?" I asked, prodding the tote with my toe. It felt heavy.

"Just four, but they're heavy going, literally and figuratively. All that spidery longhand to wade through, and it gets wobblier as Harriett ages. Thank goodness she didn't write in them every day. These go back to the 1960s. I didn't have time to do more than flip through the earliest one, but the first entry is in 1967. Mavis' daughter would have been born and given up for adoption long before that."

"Mmmmm," I agreed, "but we already know about that scandal. If Harriett did write anything about that, which I doubt, it will corroborate what Mavis told me, but that's really not what we're looking for. We need to know what *other* small-town intrigues Harriett might have documented, unintentionally giving Prudy Crane extortion fodder all these years later."

Margo nodded and sighed deeply. "So how do you want to do this? Should we split them up and each take two?"

I pulled one of the heavy, leather-bound volumes out of the tote. *Murder on the Orient Express* was imprinted on the spine, followed by the name Agatha Christie, but when I lifted the front cover, Harriett's shaky penmanship was revealed. "Interesting," I observed idly. "I wonder where she came up with the idea of false covers for her journals—and why she went to the bother of being so secretive? From what I know of her, she had very few visitors and no close friends or relatives, once Mavis left. Who was she hiding these from?"

"I haven't a clue, but she may not have had any

specific reason. I think it was just her nature to be secretive. It's a bit extreme, I admit, but some old ladies are just like that, you know. They take their girlish peccadilloes to the grave."

"If that was her intention, then why write anything down? Or at least you'd think she would have burned these things when she got up there in years, so nobody would ever get their hands on her secrets, assuming she had any."

Margo smiled. "Now that one I can answer. There are very few old people in my experience, especially women, who can bear to think of themselves as really old. Why, everybody's twenty-two years old inside their heads, Sugar, you know that! Harriett Wheeler was simply in denial about her advancin' years, just like everyone else. She probably thought she had lots of time yet before she had to give any thought to cleanin' out that old barn, which is why poor Will and Janet had such a job doin' it when they inherited the place."

I turned a few more pages, my heart sinking. "How are we ever going to get through these things quickly? And we need to do it quickly. The police are convinced that Abby's guilty," I said and paused, in case Margo had more information to offer. Apparently, she didn't. "So we need another suspect to offer them a viable alternative as fast as we can find one. If we can't find the truth, she'll have no choice but to give up Mavis and Ephraim and…," I paused for emphasis, "…Emma. She'll have to in order to buy more time." I had already told her of my suspicion that Millie Haines was actually Mavis Griswold's long-lost daughter and the contacts Emma and I had photocopied the previous evening by way of researching that possibility. "I've got all of those contacts to wade through for any possible connection to Mavis, let alone reading diaries, and there's the open house and taking Manny's aunt to the theater tonight..." I heard myself beginning to whine.

"I know, I know. We'll read as much as we can between visitors at the open house, but frankly, I don't see there bein' many lulls. Every curiosity seeker in town will turn out for this one."

"Hey, Mom, Margo," boomed a familiar voice. I looked around to see Joey waving at us as he made his way through the crowded tables to our booth. "I found your note. Looks like I'm getting cheated out of my home-cooked dinner tonight, so I thought I'd let you buy me breakfast to make up for it." He kissed Margo's cheek and ruffled my hair before sliding into the booth next to me. "Whatcha got there?" He helped himself to the last sausage on my plate and looked from one to the other of us. "Helloooo, anybody home?"

Margo and I looked at each other for a second. Then we both smiled broadly.

"Joey!" I greeted him effusively. "Did you sleep well, dear? Here, I'll get you some coffee." I waved eagerly to Sherri, who had thought we were finished and was approaching with our check. "We need another breakfast for my son, here. Anything he wants, just add it to our bill!" I snatched a menu from its holder on the table and put it in Joey's hands.

He looked at us suspiciously. "Why do I feel like a fly that just walked into a big, sticky spiderweb?"

"Got big plans for today, Sugar?" Margo inquired pleasantly. "Or do you feel like doin' a little readin' for your mama and me?"

~ * ~

By noon, Joey was hunkered down on the family room sofa with a cat tucked on either side of him, engrossed in the first of Harriett Wheeler's diaries. As a little kid, he had always been snoopy, ransacking the house for his Christmas and birthday presents, reading Emma's diaries, and that sort of thing, so I felt confident that this assignment was no hardship on him. And despite his youthful nosy streak, I had complete faith in my now adult son's ability to keep his mouth shut. It had always been the discovery of the secret that intrigued him, not blabbing it. As long as he was in the know, he was capable of remaining silent until hell froze over, I knew. Margo and I agreed that it was the perfect solution, solving our time crunch while sparing us the knowledge of anyone else's past indiscretions. Joey was under strict orders not to reveal the contents of the diaries to anyone, not even to his sister or us, unless in his judgment the documented offense was something worth paying a blackmailer to keep silent about.

As I rushed around collecting what I would need for the afternoon, I became aware of a ruckus going on outside the house and opened the front door to see what was happening. A knot of my neighbors, including self-appointed condo policewoman Edna Philpott, stood in the yard across the street. They seemed to be vigorously debating the source of a stream of water that was spouting next to the driveway. Within a minute, Edna disappeared inside along with the owner of the house. I hoped they were calling someone who would be equipped to deal with what was rapidly becoming an emergency. In the few moments I had been watching, the puddle forming in the street had grown into a small pond and was spreading rapidly in the direction of my unit. With no time to investigate the situation, I charged Joey with finding out what was going on and letting me know.

"Sorry to leave you holding the bag, but I haven't got a lot of other choices. I've got to get over to the Wheeler House. Thanks, Honey… and let me know if you have any leads for us, too," I reminded him as I headed out the door to the garage. If Manny calls, tell him I'll meet him here at five thirty. My cell phone will be on, if he needs to reach me," I added guiltily. I fished it out of my handbag and punched it on so I wouldn't forget.

"Got it. Bye." Totally engrossed, he turned another page without looking up. I took the hint and left. When I raised the garage door, I noted with alarm that the storm drains on both sides of the street were already overwhelmed, and the water level was steadily rising. The situation was not improved by the piles of leaves that had been raked into the gutters, ready for removal. The flow of the water had combined with the already sodden leaves into a thick, clogging soup. A couple of men were attempting to clear one of the drains, but it looked like a losing battle. *What else can go wrong?* I wondered and immediately regretted the thought. No doubt I would find out soon enough. I backed out cautiously and headed for Prospect Street, wondering if I would be able to get back into my driveway later in the afternoon.

When I made the final turn onto Wolcott Hill Road, I knew we were in for a hectic afternoon. The open house wasn't scheduled to begin until 1:00, but cars already lined both sides of the street, and the curious roamed freely around the yard. Some even had the nerve to climb the steps to the front porch and peer into the windows, hands shading their eyes for a clear view. Reminding myself that I was there to help Margo sell the place for Will and Janet, I bit my tongue and nodded as pleasantly as possible as I let myself in the front door. Margo had already opened the lockbox, the secure container that held the front door key that was affixed to the house's front doorknob.

Margo met me in the foyer. In time-honored realtor fashion, she had turned on nearly every light in the place to warm the place up and avoid the appearance of hiding something. Colorful brochures about the house, freshly printed at Kinko's, were fanned out on the hall table next to a stack of Margo's business cards. The brochures contained several appealing photos and basic information about the structure's age, square footage, mechanicals, property taxes, heating and electric costs, and so on. A sign-in sheet for visitors completed the display.

In the sitting room, an instant fire log burned softly in the fireplace grate, making a homey glow, and a bowl of fresh flowers graced the coffee table. From the kitchen wafted the aromas of freshly brewed coffee and something made with cinnamon warming in the oven.

"Apple crisp bars," Margo announced. "Easy to serve and not too sticky. After all our hard work yesterday, I don't want to spend the whole afternoon wiping finger marks off the woodwork. Shall we get this show on the road before the little darlings beat down the door?" She gave me a big wink, plastered a professional smile on her face, and hauled open the door.

"Hello, folks! I'm Margo Farnsworth, and this is Kate Lawrence, from MACK Realty. Come on in and sign the visitors' sheet over here, and then we'll be just tickled to answer all of your questions. Oooh, I just love that little suit you're wearin'. Very becomin'. Did you know that a famous local author lived right here in this house?"

I groaned inwardly at the effusive patter and the southern accent, both thickly applied on selling occasions, and retreated to remove the apple crisp bars from the oven and pour coffee for the crowd. In the kitchen, I was startled by the sight of half a dozen more of the curious standing in the backyard, peering up at the second floor, no doubt eager to tour the former abode of a recent murder victim. People's appetite for the details of others' misfortunes, and the gorier the better, always astounded me. I braced myself for a long afternoon.

At 3:30, my cell phone rang, and I excused myself from a woman who was clearly not a serious buyer to answer it. I stepped out the back door onto the small stoop to be able to hear myself think. So many people were crowded into the downstairs rooms that it sounded like we were having the mother of all cocktail parties. A few ghouls lingered in the back yard, including an old lady clutching a camera. She stood, unsteady but determined, snapping photos of the second floor. Was that even legal, I wondered?

"Hello, this is Kate," I said, trying to grip the tiny

telephone without pushing its volume controls, which were located maddeningly on one side where my fingers needed to be.

"So you are alive. I am glad to know it," said Armando in the haughty tone he reserved for our spats.

Oh, boy, here we go, I thought and struggled to keep my temper in check. "Yes, alive and kicking, or more accurately, trying not to *get* kicked in the crowd we have here. I'm really sorry about last night, Honey, but it simply couldn't be avoided, and you know how forgetful I am about turning on the cell phone. Anyway," I rushed on in an effort to drop that subject, "I'm looking forward to this evening. Are you picking up Estella before you get to my place, or do you want to get me first and pick her up together?"

"You still plan on attending with us, then?"

More attitude.

I tried to keep in mind that I had, in fact, stood him up the previous evening, and he had a pretty good reason to be snippy. Still, it was an effort not to throw the phone as far into the neighbor's yard as I could hurl it. I took a deep breath and let it out slowly. "Of course," I managed to say and leave it at that. There was no reason to ruin Estella's evening. We had planned this little outing for her many weeks ago, and I was sure she was anticipating it with pleasure.

"Then I will see you at the house at five. You will be ready?"

"I'll be ready," I assured him. "See you then. Oh! By the way—" Too late, I remembered about the broken water main, or whatever the problem was, on my street. I disconnected and mentally counted to ten while I considered calling Manny back. I decided against it. Joey hadn't called to deliver any particularly dire news, so the problem must have been cleared up, I reasoned. At least, I hoped so. Thank goodness Estella would be with us this evening. It was definitely going to be a good idea to have a buffer tonight. Not for the first time, I cursed Manny's tendency to pout. I far preferred a forthright, air-clearing quarrel to the icy silence he assumed on these occasions. We didn't fight often, but when we did, I always got the silent treatment for several days. Once again, I experienced doubts about moving in together. Being given the cold shoulder from a separate residence was one thing, but sharing a roof under those circumstances would be very uncomfortable.

I returned to the house, unplugged the coffee machine, and cleared away the remains of the apple crisp bars in an effort to start closing down. We had limited the open house to three hours, knowing it would be difficult to clear the house right on time, but by 4:30, we finessed the last of our visitors out the front door and closed it firmly.

"So?" I asked Margo. "Any hot prospects?"

For answer, she fanned a sheaf of buyer qualification sheets at me. "More than I've had time to count. Unless I miss my guess, while you're loungin' around at the theater tonight, I'm goin' to be up to my glorious backside in a biddin' war," she opined with satisfaction. "By this time tomorrow, Will and Janet should be off the hook. Well, speak of the devil," she finished up, peeking through the front curtains. The Copelands were venturing onto the premises at last, about to ring the doorbell when Margo threw open the door.

After saying a quick hello, I left her to deliver the good news and go through a couple of hard offers that had already been made on their property. I whizzed through both floors of the house, turning off lights and collecting paper cups and plates in a trash bag, then fled out the front door.

"Go, go!" Margo assured me. "I'll be just fine."

Not only was she fine, I knew, she was entirely in her element and having the time of her life. I made a run for it.

My heart sank at the scene that greeted me when I turned into The Birches. Several Metropolitan Water District Commission vehicles, including a pumper truck, lined the street. Floodlights shone on half a dozen men in yellow rain gear and boots. They stood on either side of a large trench in my across-the-street neighbor's yard. The flow of water had been stemmed, but the street remained clogged with sodden leaves, pieces of broken pipe and other debris. After waiting for several minutes, I was motioned ahead by one of the MWDC workers. It was just barely possible to squeeze through the trucks and maneuver into my driveway. To my surprise, Manny's car was already in the garage. I rushed up the garage stairs and yanked open the kitchen door, knowing I was late but glad, at least, to have an indisputable excuse. "I'm home!"

Armando sat at the kitchen table, a cup of tea before him, reading the newspaper. He was immaculately turned out, as always, in gray slacks, crisp blue shirt, navy sport coat, and neatly knotted silk tie. I immediately felt frumpy, but he looked up and smiled.

"So you made it." He rose and kissed my cheek. "It was a very interesting situation out there when I came in half an hour ago. Are they making any progress? Would you like a cup of tea?"

Oh, good, he's decided to quit pouting. "There's no time for tea," I said, conscious of time ticking past. "Where's Joey?" I added, noticing the silence from the family room.

Armando looked surprised. "I do not know. He was not here when I arrived."

That's odd, I thought. I tossed my briefcase on the counter and headed for my bedroom. "Just give me two minutes to freshen up, and I'll be ready to go," I threw over my shoulder. *Thank goodness for Margo's apple crisp bars, since I'm not going to get dinner any time soon.* Hurriedly, I threw off my flat shoes and blazer and ran into the bathroom to brush my teeth and re-apply lipstick. I flicked a little blusher and powder onto my cheeks, ran a brush through my hair, and spritzed on a little cologne. From the closet, I grabbed a fitted silk jacket in a royal purple color that Manny liked. It would dress up the black pants I was still wearing. I shoved my feet into strappy sandals as I buttoned the jacket. That would have to do. I checked the time. Five forty-five. We could just make it, if only we could get out of the driveway.

When I got back to the kitchen, I put food down for Jasmine and Simon, who also were nowhere to be seen. No doubt, they were hiding from all of the strange lights and sounds in the street. I plucked a light coat from the front closet and headed back out to the garage. The scene was the same as it had been a few minutes ago, but things seemed to be winding down. Several MWDC workers were shoveling dirt back into the trench they had created across the street, now that repairs had been completed. Others had fanned out into the driveways of the houses in the immediate area and were working with heavy rakes and shovels to clear them of leaves and mud.

To my surprise, Manny stood in the driveway, attempting to get the attention of the yellow-suited worker who was clearing debris in the gutter. I watched in disbelief as he snapped his fingers in the worker's direction, yelling, "Over here! You! Over here!" The man, who looked exhausted, stopped what he was doing and looked up at Manny, not understanding what he was yelling over the noise of the pumper and other trucks and workers. "There are leaves and mud here that must be removed here," Manny called imperiously. "Please attend to it immediately. It is important that we be able to exit, as we have theater tickets, and we are already late."

I couldn't believe my ears, and apparently, neither could the MWDC worker, who didn't bother to conceal his disgust for this arrogant fool who seemed to think he should care about his theater tickets. Manny wasn't aware of my presence, and I looked at the worker and shook my head slightly. Whirling on one heel, I stalked back into the garage, grabbed a rake, and took it to where Manny still stood, yelling over the truck noise. The MWDC worker had his head down, ignoring us. "Here," I yelled, thrusting the rake at Manny. "Use this."

Manny looked at me but didn't reach for the rake. "That is what *he* gets paid for," he said, and my jaw dropped.

"It will only take you a few seconds, Armando. This man doesn't work for us."

"It is what he is being paid to do right now," he insisted stubbornly as I continued to stand there, awkwardly holding the rake.

"Fine, then! I'll do it myself!" I retorted. I waded into the mess despite my leather sandals and angrily began pushing at the sodden leaves. Manny took hold of the rake.

"No, you will not do his job!"

Becoming aware that we were quarreling, the MWDC worker looked up and decided to head off further trouble. Sullenly, he lugged his rake over to where we stood and started to deal with the clog.

"Thank you," Manny said.

The man did not acknowledge him, and I didn't blame him.

I yanked the rake away from Manny. My shoes ruined, I squelched back up the driveway and hurled the rake into the garage, Manny following me closely.

I was furious. "You are being a total jackass!"

His face turned into an affronted mask, his eyes flat and cold. "In that case, I am sure you would prefer that Estella and I attend the theater without you this evening," he said stonily. Without another word, he got into his car and left, narrowly avoiding the worker still pushing at leaves and mud at the end of the driveway.

"I'm sorry!" I called to the worker, who lifted a hand to me and shrugged.

"No problem, lady," he called back. "We get guys like

him all the time."

Well, I don't. I fumed silently. *I don't get guys like him at all.*

~ * ~

An hour later, having quieted my temper in a bubble bath, I stood at the kitchen counter in baggy sweats, putting together a chicken sandwich for my supper under the watchful eyes of Simon and Jasmine. They had reappeared at the sound of the refrigerator door opening. I never knew precisely where they hid out during times of stress, but I had stopped worrying about it. When the coast was clear, all I had to do was call "Chicken!" and they rematerialized. I put some tidbits for them on a paper towel on the floor, and then sat down at the kitchen table to eat and try to sort out the events of the day. Predictably, the phone rang. Whoever it is can just leave a number, I thought irritably. I waited for my outgoing message to end so I could hear what the caller said.

"Hi, 'Cita! Guess you're out with my stepdaddy somewhere," Emma said, using the audacious nickname she used, only half in jest, for Manny. "Just wanted you to know that I'm on the job. I did computer searches on most of the names in Millie's contact file and didn't come up with anything fishy. Most of them are business contacts, customers and like that. I called everyone I could, saying I was from an insurance company and needed to check some information with her, and every single person knew her by the name of Millie Haines. Two of the people I called turned out to be relatives, and they said she'd never been married, didn't go by any other names. Anyway, got a hot date, so I'm out the door. Talk to you tomorrow.

Love you. Bye!"

By this time, I was on my feet and nearly to the phone, but she was gone. *Hot date, huh?* I racked my memory for any mention she might have made of a new love interest but came up empty. *Maybe it's Rick Fletcher,* I thought, remembering their several encounters over the past few days. Despite our verbal sparring match of the previous evening, I liked Rick very much. Whoever it turned out to be, I was glad Emma was getting out and about again. She worked far too hard for a young woman, to my way of thinking. There would be plenty of time for work in the years ahead.

I returned to the kitchen and my uneaten sandwich. I was disappointed in the results of Emma's research on Millie Haines, but realistically, what could we expect to discover? Even if she was Mavis Griswold's long-lost daughter, she would be known by relatives and customers by her adopted name. Short of hiring a private detective, I didn't know what else we could do, and even that might prove to be a dead end if the adoption papers were sealed. I had a dim recollection that adoption files in California were now searchable once the adoptee reached the age of 21, which Millie certainly was, but I couldn't remember where I'd heard that. I made a mental note to look into it tomorrow. Once again, I picked up my sandwich, and once again, the phone rang.

"Hi, Ma. Where are you? I got called into work tonight, so I didn't get all the way through—"

This time, I was faster on my feet and snatched the phone from its charger. "Joey! I was wondering where you'd gone. What did you find out so far? Where are the diaries?"

"I found out exactly nothing except a lot of silly gossip," he said with disgust. "That Harriett Wheeler must have been some piece of work. I plowed through one whole volume and half of the next one, and all I can tell you is that she was the most self-righteous, judgmental cow you can imagine. You think Philpott is bad? Trust me. You did not want to be one of Harriett Wheeler's neighbors. She didn't have one good word to say about anybody! Hang on, Ma, I've got somebody on the radio."

I mulled over what he'd said as I listened to his exchange with another trucker on the citizen's band radio Joey always had on in his cab. They went back and forth a few times about a major accident down the road and alternate routes that were still viable. Then Joey came back on the phone.

"Sorry, but I've got to get off. There's a big pile-up on I-95, as usual, and the Sunday night traffic is going to be hellacious."

"Wait, wait! Where are the diaries?" I yelled frantically before he could disconnect.

"Oh, yeah. I put them under your bed so they wouldn't be lying around in the open. I didn't know if Manny was up on this murder gig you're into. Gotta go."

"Murder gig? Hey, this isn't something I chose—" but he was gone, leaving me only marginally informed and frustrated once again. This time, when I trudged back into the kitchen, I carried the cordless phone with me. I seated myself and took an enormous bite of my sandwich. As I chewed, I thought about the unread diaries under my bed. Guess I wouldn't lack for amusement this evening after all. Somehow, the thought didn't make me feel any better. The phone rang while my mouth was still full, and I chewed frantically while my message tape played in the living room.

Margo, sounding distraught, started to speak right after the beep. "Sugar, the most distressin' thing has happened. I know you're out—"

I spit chicken and lettuce into a napkin and punched on the phone. "I'm here. Are you all right?" I said without preamble.

"Kate! I'm so glad to hear your voice." The slight tremor in Margo's voice was totally uncharacteristic, and my stomach tightened.

"Tell me."

"It's the house, the Wheeler… the Copeland—" Margo gulped.

"I know which house you mean. What about the house?" In the ensuing few seconds of silence, I could feel Margo making the effort to pull herself together.

"There was an intruder," she began again.

"An intruder? While you were still there? Are you okay?" I asked again.

"No, no, not while I was there… although earlier, I saw someone… no, it was more like I *felt* someone peekin' at me through the kitchen window." She shuddered audibly.

"Margo, where are you now? I'll throw on a raincoat over my sweats and be right there," I said. I stood up and looked around the kitchen for my purse and car keys.

"You don't have to do that, Sugar. John is here with me."

"The *police* are there? That does it. I'm on my way." I

headed for the front closet.

For the first time, Margo chuckled, sounding more like herself. "This is more in the nature of a social call, if you get my meanin', although it surely didn't start out that way. Now just be still for a minute and let me get through this."

"Okay," I said obediently and sank back into my chair, clutching my car keys.

"Here's what happened. After you left, I visited with Janet and Will for a bit, talked with them about the number of visitors we'd had, assured them we were confident of a quick sale, that sort of thing. They were happy to hear it, but they were not happy to be in that house, I could tell. So I said good night and promised to call them later this evenin'. Then I went upstairs, turned off lights, finished tidyin' up. I packed up my briefcase and went into the kitchen to put that big bag of trash out on the back porch, and that's when I saw him."

"Him?"

"The man on the back stoop, peerin' through the window at me."

"I thought you said you didn't see him."

"Well, I mean I didn't get a real good look at him. He was scrunched over with his hand half coverin' his eyes, leanin' off the stoop to look into the windows."

I imagined the scene, and a chill ran down my spine. "What did you do?"

"Why, I nearly jumped out of my skin, of course! What would you do? And then I got myself together, figurin' it was just some latecomer tryin' to get a look at the place. So I pulled open the door."

"Margo, you didn't!" I wailed. "You should have called the police!"

"Just hush up and give me a minute. So I pulled open the back door, and whoever it was almost fell off the stoop. I was standin' there ready to introduce myself, and he just ran off across the yard. He must have been dressed in dark colors, because all I could see were his big, white shoes runnin' like fury for the privet hedge that runs along the back of the yard. And then I called the police."

"Oh, great! By the time they showed up, I'm sure there was no trace of this guy, right? I'm sure it was very frightening, and I'm appalled that you opened the door to a stranger who was prowling around in the dark, but it's not like you to sound as upset as you do over something that happened hours ago. What's the rest of the story?"

"If you would just settle down, I would be more than happy to tell you," Margo snapped. She sounded more like herself with every moment, thank heaven. An intimidated Margo was unimaginable. "As it happened, John was on duty, and he took the call personally." Some muffled smoochy sounds made it past the hand with which Margo was covering the phone. I distinctly heard her giggle, but I wanted to know the rest of the story more than I wanted to know what was going on in the background.

"Margo?" Impatiently, I drummed the table with my fingernails.

"Sorry, Sugar. Like you said, when John got here, he checked everythin' out thoroughly," another giggle, "and found no trace of an intruder. So we locked the place up and left. John was gettin' off duty, so we went to have a little dinner in the South End. That's when he got the call."

"Another call?"

"Well, not from me, Silly. From the desk sergeant at the police station. While we were at dinner, the Wheeler house was broken into and ransacked, Kate. John and I went over there, and it was just awful. From the outside, it looked perfectly normal, not a thing out of place. But the inside… oh, Kate!" The tremble returned to her voice.

"What about the inside?"

"It wasn't just a burglary. There wasn't anythin' to steal, really. All the electronics had been moved out long ago. And this wasn't just vandals, kids messin' up the place for fun. This had to be the work of a crazy person, Kate. All that beautiful molding, the hardwood floors. Somebody took an axe to it, and a crowbar, and other things, too, from the look of it. The investigatin' officers said they had never seen anything like it in this town. There are great big holes punched in the walls. The kitchen cabinet doors are ripped off the hinges. The bathroom tiles are smashed. I just could not believe my eyes."

And I couldn't believe *my* ears. That beautiful old house violated in this awful way just as it was about to find a new owner who would love and enjoy it. For what reason? It made me ill to think of it.

"And nobody saw or heard anything? What about Janet and Will? Weren't they right next door while all of this was going on?"

"Well, that's the thing. Nobody heard a sound, because it was done inside with the doors and the windows all shut tight. And here's the strangest part. Technically speakin', the house wasn't broken into. When the police got there, the doors were all locked. The lock box was right where it was supposed to be on the front doorknob, and the house key was still inside it."

I put my head in my hands and tried to think. "Then who called the police to report the, uh, whatever you call this?"

"They don't know. They believe the call was made by whoever did this from right inside the house."

"That's not possible. The house line was disconnected weeks ago."

"The call wasn't made from a land line, Kate. It was made from your cell phone. You must have left it there this afternoon."

Ten

Despite my exhaustion, I slept badly. When I did doze off, it was to suffer impossibly convoluted dreams in which Manny chased yellow-suited MDC workers with a kitchen knife, and Prudy Crane refused to take my order for a cell phone, which she held just out of my reach. At 4:30 a.m. I lay awake in the dark, almost afraid to doze off again. Thinking it must be time for breakfast if I was awake, Simon butted me with his head in an effort to roll me out of bed. It was too early and too dark to gauge the weather, but I had a feeling it would be a cold, gray morning. *Good.* It would match my mood to perfection.

While the puzzled, but appreciative, cats ate an early breakfast and my coffee brewed, I stared at the tote bag into which I had repacked the four volumes of Harriett Wheeler's diaries. Despite the whirlwind of confusion that clouded my thinking about this investigation, I had come to a decision: before I did anything else this morning, I would haul Harriett's diaries to the police station and turn them over to Lieutenant Harkness and his investigators to make what use of them they might. I had had enough of Harriett's drivel and was convinced that her writings would produce no information of value. Since they began well after Mavis' and Henry's daughter had been born and given up for adoption, it seemed unlikely that any mention would be made of them in the two volumes Rick and I had not read, so I didn't feel that I was risking exposure for them. In fact, I didn't think I was risking exposure for anyone, judging from the petty, querulous entries Joey and I had already waded through. From what I could tell, all those diaries revealed was that Harriett Wheeler had been a supremely self-involved piece of work, and I doubted that would come as a surprise to anyone who had known her.

Still, someone besides us had been looking for the diaries, if I was correctly interpreting the damage done to the Wheeler house Sunday evening. How anyone else knew of their existence, I didn't know, but the damage inflicted to the walls and floorboards of the old house convinced me that the intruder was looking for something of bulk, and the diaries were the only thing we had found that fit that description. Whoever it was must have overheard me talking with Emma or Margo about them and decided to try to beat us to them. Now that they knew they had not done so, we, or at least our residences, would be in jeopardy. To head off further property damage, or possibly violence, I intended to march into the police station in full daylight, carrying the books, and emerge without them. If anyone was watching me, it would be clear that I had been in possession of the diaries but no longer was. I would tell the Lieutenant the truth, or at least a slightly modified version of it. While cleaning the house and preparing it for the open house on Sunday, we had dusted the volumes on Prudy's bookshelves. While perusing them casually, we had discovered what they really were and had appropriated them for safekeeping while deciding what to do with them. Harriett Wheeler had been something of a local celebrity, after all. The Wethersfield Library or one of the local museums might wish to add the diaries to their collections. After last night, however, it occurred to us that whoever vandalized the Wheeler house might have been searching for these very diaries, and so we were handing them over like the public-spirited citizens we were.

I didn't really expect Harkness to buy this amateurish blend of fact and fiction, but Margo had told me that John, in a rare fit of candor on this subject, had confessed his disinclination to arrest Abby Stoddard. Nobody really believed she was guilty, but based on the evidence available, although admittedly it was circumstantial, they had had to charge her. I figured that he would be glad enough to have a new source of information that he might not examine how we had come by, or even known about, the diaries too closely. Couldn't hurt, might help, was how I looked at it.

After downing two mugs of coffee, I headed for the shower and cranked the adjustable flow to maximum pressure, hoping for semi-alertness before I left the house. I stood under the stinging spray with my eyes shut and tried to put Manny's behavior of the previous evening into perspective. Maybe he had still been angry with me for standing him up. Perhaps he had had a bad day. It was possible that his grown daughter had telephoned, and they had gotten into one of their wrangles. Nah, I decided.

None of the above could possibly explain his highhandedness with the water district worker, and even if he could explain it, I couldn't excuse it. For a man who prided himself on unfailing courtesy to one and all, he had exhibited unforgivable arrogance. This time, he could pout until hell froze over, and I would count myself lucky to have escaped spending the evening with him.

The ten minutes I spent in the hot shower didn't improve either my mood or the weather, so I fluffed my short hair under the blow dryer, swiped on mascara and lipstick, and threw on a flowing tunic and pants in a subdued shade of taupe. At 5:30, as the sky was beginning to lighten, I grabbed my briefcase and the tote bag and headed for the door to the garage. Now that their bellies were full, Simon and Jasmine had no interest in my comings and goings and snored contentedly at the end of the couch in the living room, the one area of the house in which the furniture was forbidden to them. I didn't even pause to admonish them. If I chased them off, they would return two minutes after I left the house, I knew, and I limited my battles with them to the ones I had some chance of winning.

For the benefit of anyone who might be keeping tabs on me, despite the ungodly hour, I raised the garage door and made a show of walking around to the Altima's trunk, unlatching it, and stowing the bag of books. As I backed out of the driveway, I looked at the wreckage of my neighbor's lawn. The street and storm drains had been cleared of most of the debris, but that yard would have to be completely resodded. I felt eyes upon me, or perhaps I only imagined it, and took a quick look around me. I could see no one else up and about, but at The Birches, that didn't mean I wasn't being watched. I knew from long experience that there were many in the condo community whose primary recreation was monitoring the activities of their neighbors from behind concealing drapes and shades. In this instance, I welcomed their nosiness. I wanted everyone possible to know about my trip to the police station and the volumes I intended to leave there.

Slowly, I drove the length of the private access road and turned left onto Prospect Street. I would follow that a couple of miles, then turn left again onto the Silas Deane Highway. From there it was a straight shot of perhaps two more miles to the new police station.

The streets were all but deserted as I headed down Prospect toward the Silas Deane Highway. The sky was just beginning to lighten, and what few vehicles there were on the road were using headlights. In fact, the black Trans Am behind me had his high beams on, which glared annoyingly in my rearview mirror. *Too much car for his brain, obviously.* I pushed the mirror to one side until I lost the fool, just barely resisting the urge to make an obscene gesture. Where Prospect intersected with Maple, I made the dogleg to the left and started around the curve that lead down to the Deane, signaling to make a left there also, but the Trans Am abruptly pulled out from behind me and came up alongside me on the left, preventing me from moving into that lane. *What a jackass! First he blinds me with his high beams, then he changes lanes and blocks my turn.* I directed a scathing glare to my left but was unable to judge its effect, since the windows of the black Trans Am had a heavy tint—too heavy for me to see through.

Impatiently, I drummed my fingers on the steering wheel, waiting for the light to change so the Trans Am would make his turn and I could make mine. The only other vehicle in sight was an eighteen-wheeler bearing the Stop & Shop Supermarkets logo. It was approaching the intersection from the right, probably heading out after making a night delivery at the Rocky Hill store. He slowed and downshifted for the turn, then cranked hard right onto Route 3 straight ahead of me, which would lead him over the Putnam Bridge to Glastonbury. Watching the trucker, I suddenly missed Joey and wondered what highway he was negotiating right now, or was he sleeping in the snug bunk behind the seats of his rig's cab?

At long last, the light changed, and I waited for the Trans Am to get out of my way, but it didn't move. This guy was some jerk. I tooted my horn briefly and made "get moving" circles in the air with my finger, but the Trans Am didn't budge. Disgusted, I took my foot off the brake and gave the Altima some gas to move ahead of and around the Trans Am to make my turn, but the black car jumped to life and kept pace with me, forcing me to cross the Silas Deane instead of turning left. This guy was drunk or crazy or both, I decided. The Stop & Shop tractor trailer lumbered along in the right hand lane, picking up speed as he moved through the gears. As I moved past the truck, the Trans Am fell in behind me, and my annoyance turned to anger. I needed to lose this jerk, and then I had to find a place to turn around so I could head back to the Deane and be on my way.

I straightened my rearview mirror and was shocked at how closely he was following me. Instead of being blinded by his headlights, I couldn't even see them, just the black hood and tinted windshield. My hands tightened on the wheel, and the back of my neck prickled atavistically as it dawned on me that this wasn't just some yahoo playing road games with a stranger. This was deliberate. Whoever was driving the Trans Am had targeted me, and his intentions weren't good. My heart began to pound. I could never hope to outrun him, so I took the only defensive action I could devise on the fly. I cleared the truck's front bumper and, praying that the driver was paying attention, wrenched my wheel to the right to slide into his lane right in front of him. Predictably, the driver hit the air horn. I couldn't blame him, but I had bigger trouble than a pissed-off trucker right now. I was careful to maintain enough speed so that the truck didn't have to brake, but I needed his rig as a barrier behind me. To appease him a little and to let him know I was in trouble, I hit the hazard light button on the dash and pointed frantically at the driver on my left. Maybe the trucker would call the state police. In the meantime, whatever the driver of the black car had in mind, surely he wouldn't be stupid enough to take on an eighteen-wheeler.

Frustrated, the Trans Am kept pace on my left as the three vehicles crossed the two-lane bridge over the Connecticut River. I didn't know what the trucker could be thinking, but my mind worked feverishly, trying to remember the sequence of exits ahead. Then I hit on what would have to pass for a plan. As we came off the bridge,

I accelerated, catching the Trans Am by surprise, and for a moment, he was nearly parallel with the semi. The Main Street-Glastonbury exit came up on the right, and I tore onto it at breakneck speed, hoping I had timed it right and the big rig would block my pursuer from following me onto the ramp. I fought to keep control of the Altima as my own brakes locked and I slid, more than drove, into the intersection at the bottom of the ramp. Above me on the highway, the Trans Am roared into reverse, then plunged down the ramp after me. *Damn.*

I was grateful that traffic was almost nonexistent as I yanked the car left onto Glastonbury Boulevard and floored it for Main Street, for once in my life praying that a cop would spot me. At the intersection ahead of me, I could see a few cars moving along Main Street. My hands ached as I clung desperately to the wheel. I dragged it hard right and careened through the intersection, tires screaming, without lifting my foot from the accelerator.

Miraculously, I didn't hit anyone. Behind me, I heard the Trans Am scream around the corner, followed by the clash of metal on metal. He had hit something, but apparently, it wasn't enough to slow him down. I flew on down Main Street, hoping against hope that I remembered the location of the Glastonbury Police Department correctly. It was a town I seldom visited, other than to shop in its bookstores and malls. I leaned on the Altima's horn and blared through the red light at the New London Turnpike, the Trans Am gaining on me, then blew through the four-way stop at Hebron Avenue, still honking wildly. *Please, please let it be where I think it is,* I prayed.

And then I saw it, the white wooden sign on my left

and the two-story red brick building behind it. Two patrol cars were parked at the left of the long driveway, but no officers were in sight as the Altima screamed through a hard left turn but missed the driveway. A young officer emerged from a side entrance and stared in amazement as the car churned across the front lawn of the station, spitting chunks of sod behind the rear wheels. It came to rest on the pavement with its bumper barely a foot from the cruisers, for which I was insanely grateful.

Behind me, the Trans Am fared no better. Attempting to follow me into the hard left turn, the driver had missed badly, actually striking the white wooden pole holding the sign for the Police Department before screaming to a stop against a pine tree. At that point, confronted by the young officer who was now speaking rapidly into a radio, the driver must have realized where I had led him. The big motor idled for only seconds before roaring into reverse at full throttle, and the car shot backwards into Main Street. As the first officer approached my car, gun drawn, two more sprang from the police station entrance and leaped into the nearest cruiser. Siren wailing, they tore after the Trans Am. Officer number one approached the Altima cautiously, gun at the ready. He bent down and motioned for me to lower my window, and I fumbled at the buttons on the door panel until the glass went down.

"What's going on?" he demanded. Despite his steely eyes, I couldn't help thinking that he didn't look old enough to carry the gun at his side. For some reason, this struck me as hilarious. I sat bolt upright, both hands visible on the steering wheel, and laughed and laughed until I cried.

~ * ~

Once my bout of hysteria had passed, Officer Petrillo could not have been nicer to me if I had been his mother. He quickly relayed the information I gave him to his colleagues in pursuit of the Trans Am, and then helped me out of the car and into the police station. The dispatcher relayed word of a 911 call made by the Stop & Shop trucker about a woman in an Altima who was being pursued by a black Trans Am. There had been another call from a local octogenarian whose sedan had been sideswiped near the highway entrance by a fishtailing black car, make and model unknown. The old gent had been heading out early "to beat the traffic" and was very shaken up by the incident. I knew exactly how he felt. And then, of course, there was the eyewitness report of Officer Petrillo, who had watched me and my tormenter arrive across the front lawn of the station. I wondered how much I was going to owe the Town of Glastonbury for the sod and the sign, although technically speaking, the sign hadn't been my fault.

After settling me in an interview room with a Styrofoam cup of coffee, Office Petrillo asked me to write out my statement in longhand, a procedure with which I was becoming dismayingly familiar. I limited my comments to the events of the morning, making no reference to the Wethersfield homicide investigation. Although I felt strongly that the two things were connected, I couldn't say so for certain, so why get into it? I said simply that for reasons known only to the other driver, whose face I was unable to see because of the heavily tinted windows on the Trans Am, I had been harassed and chased as witnessed by the Stop & Shop trucker and the other motorists I had narrowly avoided hitting. So far, the Trans Am had eluded the pursuing officers, but based on the information provided by the observant, however rattled, truck driver, an APB was being issued as we spoke. I had every confidence that the driver would soon be apprehended, and after that, we'd see where we were. When Officer Petrillo asked where I had been headed at that hour of the morning, I'd said simply that I was headed for my place of business to get a jump on the day. Except for one final turn, the route I had planned to take to the police station was identical to the one I took every morning to MACK Realty.

Presently, the officer excused himself to deliver my statement to a clerical person, who would transcribe it for my review and signature, and to check on my car. I was content to sip my coffee and stare blankly at the wall during his absence. When he returned, he reported that the Altima had been parked properly at the side of the driveway and seemed to be just fine. Not even a tire had been blown, although I'd probably want to have someone look them over more thoroughly when I had a chance. Nobody mentioned the tote bag full of mystery novels, so I assumed the trunk hadn't been opened. Even if it had been searched, such reading material would be considered entirely suitable for a single lady of my age, I was sure.

After perhaps twenty minutes, Officer Petrillo placed a computer print-out of my statement on the table in front of me. I read it and signed it. In response to his question, I assured him that I felt able to drive. He promised to keep me informed on the progress of their investigation and ushered me out the side entrance I had entered just hours before, where the Altima waited placidly in a visitor parking space. Except for muddy tires, it looked exactly as it always did.

    I started to think that perhaps the events of the morning had all been a bad dream, but one look at the ruined lawn snapped me back to reality. When I put them on the wheel, my hands felt bruised and tender. I flipped down the visor and was surprised to see how normal I looked. I had chewed off my lipstick, but there was nothing unusual about that. The tremble in my fingers, as I attempted to reapply it, was the only vestige of my harrowing experience. I looked at my watch and was shocked to see that it was only 8:05 a.m. It felt as if a week had passed since I stood in my kitchen drinking coffee, but despite the harrowing events of the morning so far, I wouldn't even be especially late to work.

    I drove sedately over the bridge back to Wethersfield, happy to remain within the speed limit, and considered my options. I couldn't prove it, but I every instinct told me that my stalker had been attempting to force me off the road this morning in order to get his hands on the diaries in my trunk. That meant he had to have watched me leave The Birches. Joey and I had read only two of the four volumes so far, and despite our doubts, it was certainly possible that something incriminating remained to be discovered. Presumably, the driver of the Trans Am thought so and had trashed the Wheeler house for the same reason. Otherwise, more than one violent thug was after Harriett's scribblings, and that seemed extremely unlikely.

Thwarted in both attempts, the stalker had to be murderous by now, so good sense would dictate that I turn the diaries over to the police and advance that theory as quickly as possible, right? On the other hand, my would-be assailant was well on his way to being apprehended, thanks to the quick action of the Glastonbury police, so I had little to fear for the moment. Would it not be more effective—and helpful to Abby's cause—to wade through the remaining two diaries ourselves and present Lieutenant Harkness with an alternative suspect, based on what we learned?

I drove along the Silas Deane Highway to the intersection of Old Main Street and pondered what to do while waiting for the light to change. Straight through would lead me to the police station. A right turn would lead me to the Law Barn. The light changed, and I turned right.

As soon as I rounded the first curve, I could see parking would be a problem today. I remembered that the public hearing on the proposed smoking ban was scheduled for 7:00 p.m. at the Keeney Memorial, diagonally across the street from our offices. Already, the protestors paced the length of the block, cigarettes dangling defiantly from mouths and fingers, signs held high. "Smokers have rights, too," seemed to be the slogan of choice today, and there were chants and shouts, as well. As I waited behind stalled drivers, most of whom were seeking nonexistent parking spaces, I could see that not all of the noise emanated from the smokers. Those in favor of the proposed ban, including several small business owners, were staging a counter-rally on the opposite side of the street. Several brandished signs of their own, reading, "We don't need no stinking cigarettes!" and "Kissing a smoker is like licking an ashtray" and similarly charged slogans.

At Garden Street, I turned left, then right, to tuck the Altima into the service alley at the back of the Law Barn. Chances were I'd be blocked in before 10 o'clock, but I didn't know what else to do with it. I locked the car doors carefully, selected the two unread diaries from the bag in the trunk, and let myself into the back yard quietly through the gate in the chain link fence. Rhett Butler was already in his pen, gnawing on a bone big enough to be the hip joint of a bull moose. He looked up barely long enough to woof politely before returning to it. Margo and Kate sat on the back stairs, holding Dunkin' Donuts cups and giggling conspiratorially. No doubt they were comparing notes on the intricacies of dating police officers, if Emma had been out with Rick Fletcher last evening, as I suspected.

"Well, hey, Sugar! My, don't we look cranky this mornin'," Margo greeted me. "After my ordeal last night, Emma's been consolin' me, and I can't have you stealin' her attention with that long face of yours. What's the matter? Are you and Manny fussin' again? Now that I come to think of it, what were you doin' at home when I called you last night?"

But Emma's attention had already been diverted. One look at my face, and she was on her feet and coming toward me. "Momma?" She pulled me to her in a quick hug, and then released me to arms' length to study my face. "What is it? What's happened?"

"Speaking of ordeals," I began and launched into a five-minute recap of how my planned trip to the Wethersfield Police Station had ended on the front lawn of the Glastonbury Police Station instead. Halfway through my recitation, Emma relieved me of my handbag and the diaries and pushed me gently onto the stoop next to Margo, who wordlessly handed me the rest of her coffee. As I talked, their eyes grew round, and their mouths sagged open, but they didn't interrupt me until I had finished. Then they looked at each other and back at me. Emma's eyes were brimming dangerously.

"Well, shit, Sugar, how am I supposed to compete with that?" Margo demanded. "You have totally upstaged me and just *ruined* my day. You always were a prima donna, Kate Lawrence," she flounced, hands on hips.

Emma's tears vanished instantly as she turned to glare at my old friend, but I roared with laughter. It was just what I needed, and I howled and clapped with glee until Emma got the joke and grinned along with Margo. As we collected our cups and books and headed inside, an angry chattering came from above Rhett's pen. We shaded our eyes and looked into the lower boughs, where Fat Squirrel perched, his cheeks stuffed with peanuts. As we watched, he hurled a shell at us and scolded some more.

"No worse for wear," I noted sourly, but Emma was thrilled to see the little fleabag. I had to admit, I was glad to see him, too, albeit with reservations. Even Rhett seemed pleased to see his old adversary and looked up from his bone to pant doggily at the squirrel. Having re-established relations, F.S. scooted down the tree trunk and skittered over to the trash cans, twitching nervously. "Is he about to do what I think he's about to do?" I asked Emma. She shrugged and turned her hands palm up, and we all trooped inside.

From the lobby, the noise from both sets of demonstrators was even more audible, and it was clear that little business would be accomplished today. I, for one, was grateful. Emma retreated to the loft to reschedule the few appointments she had. After that, she would concentrate on the third of Harriett Wheeler's diaries, while I scoured the fourth one for any possible clue to the identity of Prudy's killer. Margo would spend the day running interference for us both, with the help of Jenny, who had been dropped off several blocks away and hiked in to work.

Despite all of the tea and coffee I had consumed, my eyes were heavy. I also had a killer headache. I decided to repair to the reading room, which seemed entirely appropriate to the task at hand, and nipped into the coatroom as soon as Jenny went to make some copies. Emma had given me her cell phone, since mine was still in the Wethersfield P.D.'s evidence locker, on which either she or Margo would call me if I were truly needed. "And don't turn it off!" she admonished me before scooting up to her lair.

I regarded the thing with distaste. It being Emma's phone, no doubt the thing would ring all day. I located the ring volume controls on the side and muted the ring, then laid it carefully on the mahogany vanity. I assuaged my conscience by promising myself to check messages every so often. Before sinking into the overstuffed arm chair with my reading assignment, I swallowed two Advils from the emergency stash and splashed cool water on my hands and face. Then I turned on the table lamp and sat down. I removed the cap from the listening tube so that I could monitor activity in the lobby, in case Jenny needed some help. The phone rang occasionally, but she didn't seem to be having any difficulty handling the calls.

Hoping my headache would take the hint and leave, I lifted the cover on what looked like Dorothy Sayers' *The Nine Tailors* but was actually volume four of The Wheeler Chronicles, as we had come to think of them. Based on the dates of the first and last entries, this one appeared to cover the period of eight years before Harriett's death in 2004. I sighed and struggled to focus on the spidery penmanship, which described in self-pitying tones the abuse she had had to endure at the hands of an unnamed neighbor. Apparently, the neighbor encouraged his dog to relieve himself, during their regular walks, on Harriett's lawn. I'll just bet he did, I thought groggily but pushed on to the next entry and the next.

By the time the ibuprofen worked its magic on my headache, I had slogged through three years of the same sort of petty complaints and was no closer to finding a solution to Abby Stoddard's dilemma. I decided to reward myself with a little nap before taking on 1999's entries and fell asleep almost instantly to the continuing chants of the demonstrators outside the Law Barn, which seemed to be escalating in intensity.

When I awoke, much refreshed, an hour or so later, I picked Harriett's diary back up to return to my reading. Immediately, the name "Abigail Stoddard" leaped off the page. I pushed myself fully upright and peered closely at the shaky handwriting. The date of the entry was September 16, 1999, almost exactly six years ago. Frank Wainwright had still been alive then and running The Village Diner.

It has become apparent that F.W. and tacky little Abigail Stoddard are living in sin in that man's abode. This comes as no surprise. One can hardly blame the man in these circumstances, men being the weak creatures that they are. What is terribly surprising is the involvement of M.D. in an apparent ménage a trois, something of which I would not have thought even Abigail capable. How best to deal with this news? Surely there is a town ordinance against so many unrelated people living under the same roof. Perhaps an anonymous letter to the mayor's office will put an end to this unorthodox and thoroughly offensive establishment. If not, more drastic measures may be required.

I paused to consider who "M.D." might be. A physician? Someone with those initials? The only person who came to mind was Miriam Drinkwater, the part-time curator of the Keeney Memorial, but I simply could not get my mind around the possibility of meek, self-effacing Miriam involved in a love triangle with Abby and Frank. Beyond the local business owners here in Old Wethersfield, I was acquainted with only a few dozen of the town's residents. Perhaps the telephone book would provide some clues. I put my ear to the listening tube to try to determine Jenny's location, but silence reigned. I eased out of the reading room and went in search of Margo, a phone book, and food, not necessarily in that order. Suddenly, I was starving.

Carrying the diary with me, I headed for the MACK Realty office on the other side of the lobby, but before I got there, Jenny burst through the front door of the Law Barn, bringing a wave of chanting voices and honking horns with her.

"Food!" she called cheerfully, undoing the shoulder straps of her backpack and dropping it on her desk. With her usual resourcefulness, she had realized that we were all pretty much trapped in the Law Barn until the crowds eased, helped herself to petty cash, and hiked down the street to the Diner, returning with an assortment of overstuffed sandwiches and side salads. Margo and Emma materialized instantly, and we fell upon the food like wolves, washing it down with bottles of Snapple and soda from the office refrigerator.

After several minutes of intense chewing and swallowing, Margo, Emma and I sat in a row on the lobby sofa and made sounds of contentment. With our heartfelt thanks ringing in her ears, Jenny scraped together the empty wrappings and trundled a full trash bag out back to add to Fat Squirrel's pickings for the evening and say hello to Rhett Butler. I took advantage of her absence to show Margo and Emma the diary entry that had captured my attention.

"So what do you think? Who is M.D.?" I asked after each of them had frowned over the entry for a minute. "The only name I can come up with is Miriam Drinkwater, but surely, there must be a hundred people in town with those initials. And of course, nothing says the person has to be from Wethersfield."

"Except that Harriett Wheeler knew this person, and

Harriett rarely left her house, let alone Wethersfield," Margo pointed out reasonably enough.

I could see the wheels turning in Emma's head. "Just because that awful Wheeler woman assumed there was some sort of kinky threesome going on doesn't mean there actually was, you know. All we can assume from what we see here is that the three of them were living in the same house. Maybe they had a roomer to help with expenses, or maybe Abby or Frank had a cousin or another relative staying with them for some reason. There are a dozen perfectly proper explanations for the arrangement." She stopped and looked from one to the other of us. "Don't you think?"

Margo chuckled. "This child of yours does all right in the logic department, I'm thinkin'. Must have gotten those genes from her daddy."

I threw my Snapple cap at her. "Well, the only sure way to learn the identity of M.D. is to ask Abby who was living with her and Frank in the fall of 1999, and that's what I plan to do right now. Emma, did you find anything in the diary you're reading yet?"

"Nothing, and believe me, I read every nauseating word. What a loser that woman was! I can't believe she wrote romance novels. There wasn't an ounce of romance in her soul. She was judgmental and vindictive." She shook herself and got to her feet. "Anyway, I don't think any of us has a prayer of getting our cars out of here tonight. The police have their hands full trying to keep a lid on the crowd until the hearing begins at seven."

"Crowd?" Margo and I asked simultaneously. We all got up and went to the big front doors, which Emma pulled open with a flourish. To our astonishment, the parking area out front was jammed with badly parked cars of every description, and the sidewalk now teemed with angry citizens, all of whom seemed to be yelling. A harassed young officer attempted to reason with two elderly demonstrators who were in each other's faces, one burly hand flat against each of the men's chests to hold them apart.

"That looks like Rick Fletcher's partner from the other night," I said. "Officer Chaplain or something. I cannot believe how young these policemen are getting to be."

"Ron Chapman," Emma said, "and he's thirty-one. I think I'll go say hello when he gets these old coots separated. We haven't had a chance to talk since last night."

"Last night? You mean this is who you were out with last night… the 'hot date,' if I recall your message correctly? I was sure it was Rick Fletcher."

Both Emma and Margo gaped at me for a two-count, then collapsed into hysterical laughter. "She thought it was Rick Fletcher," Margo gasped, holding her sides and wiping her eyes. Emma wasn't much better off.

"Rick Fletcher!" she hooted, leaning on the nearest car for support. "Wait until I tell Joey that you thought I was on a date with Rick Fletcher!"

I folded my arms across my chest. "And what's wrong with Rick Fletcher? I always thought he was an exceptionally nice young man. Obviously, I thought you did, too," I said, a little miffed and more than a little puzzled.

Finally, Emma took pity on my perplexity. "You really

don't know, do you?" she gasped when she could breathe again. I remained silent but raised one eyebrow. Emma looked at Margo for support. "You tell her. I don't have the heart."

Margo straightened out her face and came to give me an apologetic hug. "You poor darlin', you are absolutely right. Rick Fletcher is a delightful young man and has the makings of an extraordinary police officer, John tells me. He is also gayer than springtime, Sugar." She gave me a pitying look, then threw up her hands and hooted with laughter all the way back through the lobby to our office.

"Sorry, 'Cita," Emma comforted me. "I think it's a generational thing. Women of your age just don't seem to have the same radar we do now, although come to think of it, Margo picked up on it right away… oops! Sorry again." She gave me a hasty pat and headed out into the crowd.

"Ask Officer Macho there what's going on with the Wheeler house break-in," I yelled after her. "The Copelands are getting anxious." Emma waved in acknowledgment and was gone into the crowd. I went back inside and pulled the doors firmly shut. At this rate, we'd have half the town traipsing through the office looking for a bathroom.

~ * ~

At some point during the afternoon, the phones stopped ringing. Emma had never returned from her visit to the good looking Officer Chapman, and Margo had collected Rhett Butler and made her way, however Margo managed these things, to the Copelands' house on Wolcott Hill Road to review their situation and find out what she could about the investigation. That left Jenny and me holding the fort.

Shortly after 5:00, I finished volume four of The Wheeler Chronicles where I still sat on the lobby couch and closed the cover. I had found only one additional entry concerning Abby Stoddard and the mysterious M.D., but it was particularly vitriolic. In late November, 2002, Harriett had written,

It has been more than three years, and that filthy harlot continues to live with two men without benefit of marriage to either one. Why this immoral living arrangement is tolerated in a supposedly Christian community, I cannot understand. Now that the Blue Laws that protected us from this sort of thing have vanished along with our sacred day of rest, no decent person can consider herself safe from such abhorrent influences. My continued protests have fallen on deaf ears. I must take matters into my own hands.

There were no entries for the remainder of that year and a good part of the next. When they resumed in late 2003, they were in handwriting so shaky as to be almost illegible and consisted primarily of complaints about her deteriorating health and the general incompetence of the medical profession. By then, Harriett must have been experiencing symptoms of the illness that had claimed her life two years later.

I stood up and stretched luxuriously, working the kinks out of my shoulders and neck. What action had she taken in 2002, I wondered, and who was M.D.? There was only one sure way to find out. I would have to ask Abby.

"Jenny," I said as she was extracting a windbreaker and her sneakers from her backpack preparatory to leaving, "when you were at the diner earlier, did you happen to see Abby Stoddard?"

Jenny thought about it as she tied her shoes. "I didn't actually see her, but she was there, back in the kitchen. Deenie had her hands full trying to take orders and cover the cash register and take-out and everything else, and Abby was trying to help out with the cooking. As a matter of fact, I'm going back there now to give Deenie a hand. She must be whipped by now, and there's no point in my trying to catch a ride out of Old Wethersfield until that hearing starts at seven, and people move inside off the street."

That was good of her, I thought. "Couldn't Mort help out at the register or something? I know Abby has had a tough time trying to hire a replacement for Prudy, but surely Mort must be able to do something around there besides sweep up and fill saltshakers."

"I didn't see Mort today," Jenny said, getting to her feet and heading for the back door. "Guess he couldn't make it in with all this traffic. He wouldn't want to risk getting a scratch on that precious Trans Am of his. I'm going out the back way and cut down the service alley. See you in the a.m." She hitched her backpack over one shoulder and was gone, completely unaware of the lightning bolt she had tossed at me so casually.

For a few seconds, I was too stunned to move. Then I sank back down to the sofa, my head reeling. *Mort... Mort... What is his last name?* And then I had it. Mort Delahanty. *M.D.* This could not possibly be a coincidence. The initials in Harriett's diary, the fact that he owned a Trans Am... it was all connected, but how? I wished that

Margo and Emma were around so I could hash this all out with them. I needed to make some sense of it before I brought the diary to the police.

Mort Delahanty has been at the diner for as long as I could remember, which admittedly wasn't all that long. His role was unclear. My impression was that he suffered from some sort of mental handicap, but I had no idea what that might be. He just seemed sort of slow-witted, but I was too busy wondering why Abby tolerated Prudy Crane's surliness and inefficiency to wonder why she kept Mort Delahanty employed, as well. I had never heard him in conversation with Abby or anyone else, for that matter, but then, why would I have? Whenever I was in there, it was to pick up something quick to take back to the office. I really had no inkling of Mort's relationship with Abby or with Prudy Crane either. Still, he had access to the premises, including the chlordane and the kitchen knives, and he might very well have known about Prudy's extracurricular activities. Maybe he was her partner in crime and did away with her to keep all the blackmail money to himself. Or maybe he had known that Prudy was blackmailing Abby, as well, and had killed her out of some kind of obsessive loyalty to his kind employer.

The only thing I was certain of was that it had been Mort Delahanty in that Trans Am this morning. Vignettes of the past few days popped into my aching head… Mort's face when I had appeared at the diner to talk with Abby at her request … the open windows in Mavis Griswold's sitting room and Millie Haines' office, under which anyone might have been lurking and listening… Mort waiting at the cash register in Marsh's Pharmacy while Ephraim ranted behind the far-from-soundproof partitioning. He had probably been following me for days, but why? If he had been listening at the door outside Abby's office and heard enough to know that she had asked for my help, he would know that's what I'd been trying to do. But if he had heard only a few words at a time, an out-of-context phrase or two, he might easily have misconstrued the situation and thought I meant to do Abby harm. That was, after all, how rumors got started. A small distortion here, a slip of the tongue there, and you had a full-blown scandal in next to no time.

Scandal. I rubbed my eyes and tried to connect the dots. According to the vicious tripe served up in her diaries, scandal had been Harriett Wheeler's *raison d'etre*. She lived it, breathed it, was constantly on the alert for the possibility of it—and when none was forthcoming, she fabricated it. Now that I had seen what Harriett had implied about Abby and Frank and Mort in her diaries, I knew in my heart that it was Mort who had been trying to get his hands on the volumes in the trunk of my car, just as I was certain it was he who had vandalized the Wheeler house on Sunday night. He probably just walked in with the crowd and hid in a closet or the basement or something until Margo left. I shuddered to think of her there alone in the house with someone who was so obviously deranged.

Alone in the house. Suddenly, I was very aware of how alone I was in the Law Barn. Despite the noise of the crowd outside, the silence within was palpable, and I was sure that nobody out there would hear me if I needed help. I jumped to my feet and grabbed the phone on Jenny's desk. The number for the police department was prominently displayed on a small card taped to its side, and I wasted no time punching it in. Judging from the number of uniforms I had seen on the street earlier, the female officer who answered the phone must have been equally lonely in the station house. I explained that, due to the crowds and traffic, I was effectively trapped in the Law Barn on Old Main Street, but I needed to speak with Lieutenant Harkness or Officer Fletcher immediately in connection with the Crane investigation. I gave her the Law Barn number, and she promised to do her best to contact one or the other of them.

"Are you all right, ma'am?" she asked, concern in her voice. "You're the lady who was involved in that high speed chase in Glastonbury this morning, aren't you?"

I admitted that I was. I guess gossip travels fast in police circles, as well.

"I'm fine for the moment," I said sturdily, by way of whistling in the dark, which it literally was now. I snapped on the desk lamp and gazed fearfully around the shadowed lobby. "I know how pressed the department is right now with this hearing tonight, but I'd appreciate hearing from the lieutenant or Rick Fletcher as soon as possible."

"You've got it," she promised and disconnected.

Okay, then. It was just a matter of hunkering down and waiting. A glance at my watch told me it was nearly six. Margo was busy with the Copelands, but I felt sure that she would return at some point, if she could make her way back through the crowds. The hearing would begin in a little more than an hour, and then surely, I would hear from John or Rick or one of the other officers who were on duty in the area.

I tried to think logically. The first thing to do was to make sure no one who didn't have legitimate business here could enter the Law Barn. Margo and Emma and Millie Haines all had keys. I screwed up my courage and walked purposefully to the back entrance. As I reached for the doorknob, I noticed that my hands shook at little, but after the day I'd had, not to mention three or four extra servings of caffeine, that wasn't surprising. After turning on the floodlights, I took hold of the knob and yanked open the door. I forced myself to step onto the small back stoop to be sure nobody was lurking around the building. Standing on tiptoe and craning my neck, I could just see the roof of the Altima in the service alley. It was somehow reassuring to see that it was still there.

All was calm in the back yard, and I quickly returned inside. I threw the deadbolt on the sturdy wooden door and left the back lights on as an added deterrent to unwelcome visitors. Then I went into Millie Haines' office and checked to be sure her window was closed and locked. For good measure, I closed the door to her office and pulled a carton of copier paper in front of it. If anyone did break in through the window, I would hear it when the door thumped the carton of paper and have time to escape out the front.

Next, I checked the front door to be sure it was secure. In addition to the modern dead bolt, the door boasted an old fashioned plank-and-brackets barrier, which was never used but made an interesting decorative touch. I tested it out and found that the plank fit smoothly within the sturdy wooden brackets at either side of the door. Short of using a battering ram, no one was coming through that door tonight. There were no windows at the front of the first level, so I had no worries there.

Just for good measure, I climbed the stairs to the loft and checked things out up there. The hamster cage by Emma's desk stood empty, for once, and the law offices were unusually quiet as well. I took a good look around, even sticking my head into the office of Jimmy Seidel, phantom lawyer. I flipped on the light in his office and wondered, not for the first time, how the man managed to run a business when he was never around. *Because he has Emma*, I answered myself. Without her, this business would have folded long ago. I wondered if he was aware of that. She kept the whole place going, almost single-handedly. She even kept the plants in his office watered so the poor things wouldn't die of neglect. While I was thinking in that vein, I noticed that the potted pothos on the corner of Jimmy's desk, one of the most death-defiant plants on the face of the earth, had several yellow leaves and went over to investigate. Sure enough, the dirt was dry as a bone.

I located the water pitcher Emma kept on the credenza behind her desk and trudged back down the stairs to fill it from the visitors' bathroom. Halfway back up the stairs with the filled pitcher, I heard the distinctive sound of the light switch in Jimmy's office clicking off. The space above me went dark, and I froze where I stood. For fully thirty seconds I stood stock still, every sense straining to come up with some logical reason why I had heard what I heard and seen what I'd seen. Only one presented itself. I did not want to accept it, but ultimately, I had no choice. For who knows how long, someone else had been in the Law Barn with me, someone who did not want me to see him.

Unless I was very much mistaken, I had just taken elaborate pains to lock myself in with Prudy Crane's murderer.

Eleven

For a few more seconds, my thoughts skittered around aimlessly. Then the confusion lifted, and I knew exactly what to do. Almost calmly, I set the pitcher of water down on the step above me and turned around as quietly as I could. If Mort Delahanty was up there, he wasn't anxious for me to discover him, or he would have made his move when I let myself into Jimmy's office. If he had intended to harm me, he easily could have overpowered me there, but he had remained hidden and silent. When he heard me go back down the stairs, he must have assumed I wasn't coming back. He had no way of knowing that I intended to return to water Jimmy's plant. Obviously, he was hoping I would finally lead him to what he had been after for days, if not weeks. The diaries, I thought wearily. *He's here for the damned diaries.*

I pictured the last volume of Harriett's chronicles lying face up where I had dropped it on the couch in the lobby. How long had Delahanty been in the Law Barn? It would not have been especially difficult to enter unseen. Jenny had been absent from the lobby for long stretches, as had the rest of us, for one reason or another throughout the day. He could easily have slipped in the back door when we were all out front after lunch and nipped up the stairs to conceal himself in one of the many nooks and crannies the old structure afforded. Perhaps he had recognized my car in the service alley and decided that I had the diaries with me inside.

Suddenly, I was tired to the bone of the whole situation. To hell with the diaries, I thought. *If that's what he wants, let him have the one on the couch. I don't care anymore. It's not worth dying for.* My next thought was that at least one person, and possibly more, had already died. As quietly and quickly as I could manage it, I slipped off my shoes and descended the last few steps, keeping close to the wall to minimize the creaking of the old planks. Crossing the softly lit lobby, I scurried into the coatroom and fumbled for the pressure point on the paneling behind the coat rack. My fingers located it by instinct, and the door popped open silently. Two more seconds, and I was safely within the secret room. I knew that the lamplight would not be visible under the door, because Margo and I had checked that out, but I was still reluctant to turn it on.

I sat in the easy chair in the dark, my knees pulled up to my chest, and waited for my heart to stop thundering while I considered what to do next. Too bad my cell phone was still being held as evidence. For once, the annoying device would have come in very handy. Then I remembered that I had Emma's phone, and it was right here in the reading room with me. Best of all, Delahanty had no way of knowing about my sanctuary, so I was perfectly safe as long as I stayed in here. I could call the police, Margo, and anybody else I felt like calling, and just sit here and wait for them to come and rescue me. My relief was almost palpable.

I remembered that I had muted the phone and set it on the edge of the vanity cabinet while I read. Moving carefully, I stood up and shuffled in the direction of the vanity, moving my outstretched hands from side to side. I located the edge of the cabinet and felt gingerly along its surface until I felt the contours of the little phone. I clutched at it gleefully—and dropped it from a height of four feet onto the tiles surrounding the base of the cabinet, where it bounced and spun to a stop. *No!* I dropped to all fours and felt carefully around me. I felt the edge of the carpet, the coolness of the tile flooring, and then the pieces of what used to be Emma's phone. She's going to kill me, I thought, if Mort Delahanty doesn't get to me first and save her the trouble.

At this point, Rational Kate stepped up to assess the situation. *Just look at yourself, crawling around in the dark on your hands and knees at your age so some obsessed halfwit won't find you in a place he has no way to know even exists. Get hold of yourself. Margo and Emma are safely out of the way. Lieutenant Harkness and Rick Fletcher will check things out when you don't answer the telephone. There are about a thousand people right outside the front door. Turn on the table lamp before you break a leg, sit down like a big girl, and wait for help to arrive.* I imagined the picture I must have made creeping about on the floor and started to giggle. Then I took my own advice and groped my way back to the chair, sat in it, and snapped on the lamp. Warm light bathed the little room, and I felt calmer immediately. I looked at my watch. Six thirty. It wouldn't be long now.

Rustling sounds in the vicinity of my left ear reminded me that I had left the listening tube uncapped. If I listened carefully, maybe I could tell what Delahanty was up to in the lobby. If he found the diary on the couch, maybe he would just take it and leave. I pressed my ear to the opening hopefully. Sure enough, I could hear cautious footfalls crossing the lobby from the stairs. By cupping my hand around my ear, I could make out the rustling of papers. He must be at Jenny's desk, right beneath the other end of the listening tube, where it was hidden by the hideous self-portrait. Silence for a few seconds, and then the careful footsteps began again, this time heading away from the desk. A pause, then a grunt of satisfaction, followed by the sound of turning pages. He had found the diary.

Now that Delahanty had found what he had been seeking so desperately, I considered what he might do with it, but I didn't have to wonder for long. The sound of pages being torn violently from their binding filtered into my ear, then crumpling and more tearing. I wasn't worried. Both Margo and Emma had seen not only the diary but the precise entries that seemed to implicate Delahanty in some ancient scandal, so it wouldn't be Mort's word against mine. If it came down to it, it would be him against all three of us, so let him destroy the thing. It mattered not to me. Silence followed the ripping and tearing. Then I heard a familiar, raspy clicking that I could not quite identify at first. A few seconds more, and it came to me. It was the sound of a cigarette lighter, like the little Bic I had used years ago in my smoking days. Mort was going to burn the diary, then. But where? I hadn't heard the sound of Jenny's metal wastebasket being dragged from underneath her desk to make a receptacle for the blaze. I hadn't heard anything except ripping and tearing, followed by the clicking of the lighter. *So where was this fire being set?*

I cupped my hand more tightly around my ear as little prickles of alarm started up again on the back of my neck. The Law Barn was old and was constructed primarily of wood. We were forever being inspected by fire officials and representatives of our insurance company to be sure the appropriate number of functioning fire extinguishers, automatic sprinklers and other precautions were in place. Despite all that, we were very aware of the fire hazard presented by the old tinderbox and made sure that any smoking of cigarettes or pipes took place outside near containers of sand provided for the butts. That was one of the reasons that Jimmy and all of us at MACK Realty were solidly in favor of the proposed smoking ban. How ironic it would be if the Law Barn were torched by a cigarette lighter on the night of the hearing on a no-smoking ordinance.

After a minute or so of silence, I heard more paper being torn and crumpled, much more than Delahanty could have ripped out of the diary. The phone book, I thought, or maybe files extracted from Jenny's desk drawers. I heard one after the other of them being yanked open, and then the file cabinet behind her desk. *Was the man building a bonfire in our lobby?* Immediately, I knew that was precisely what he was doing. Whatever flame retardancy the old sofa had once had must be gone long since, so it would make a lovely base on which to heap even more combustible materials. Having lit the pile with his cigarette lighter, he would have little trouble feeding the flames with the materials readily available around him. I pictured him in a frenzy of arson, destroying Jenny's beautifully kept files in the growing flames. How long, I wondered, before he was satisfied with his work and left the building so that I could escape from my hiding place?

After what seemed like an eternity, but was probably only a few minutes, the footsteps resumed, but not in the direction of the back door, as I had supposed. Instead, they were headed for the front of the building, away from the listening tube. He must truly be mad to make his exit in full view of that crowd. Smoke would have to be billowing by now, and when he threw open the front door, the draft of air would accelerate the fire enormously. I left my chair and put my ear to the crack of the door, hoping to hear him exit. A sudden banging on the door startled me so that I fell backwards and narrowly missed hitting my head on the edge of the vanity.

"I know you're in there!" he growled fiercely, pounding the door again for emphasis. "You won't be getting up to any more of your mischief, Missus. It's done now, all done, you hear me?" A final smack.

Then I heard him dragging the coat rack away from the door. Already full of adrenaline, my heart racing, I braced myself to fight for my life. If he knew about the reading room, he must know how to get into it. I probably wouldn't win, but I'd go down fighting, I promised myself. I'd want Emma and Joey to know that I fought like hell.

But the door didn't open. Instead, I heard him grunting with effort as he heaved and pushed something solid and heavy through the coatroom and jammed it against my door. My god, he was barricading the door with Jenny's desk. I was going to burn to death in this tarted-up bathroom unless I could find some way to attract the attention of the crowd just outside the building.

"Help!" I screamed futilely, unable to fight the hysteria that rose in my chest. "Please help me somebody!" I pounded on the door, the walls, any surface I could reach, on the chance that part of the wall was hollow enough for sound to penetrate. "You've got to help me… I'm trapped in the Law Barn!"

In desperation, I began tearing books from the bookshelves next to the chair. Maybe the wall was thinner behind them. I peered between the empty shelves and saw something that resembled a doorbell. I must be delusional as well as hysterical. With absolutely nothing to lose, I pushed it. With a protesting groan of long un-oiled hinges, the entire set of shelves popped open on one side and slowly swung open, revealing what looked like a shallow closet. Cold, night air huffed in from the plank wall beyond, which must have been a door at one time. Instinctively, I moved toward it and put my mouth against a crack.

"Help me!" I screamed again, my voice hoarse and failing. Once more, I pounded on the wall.

To my astonishment, my plea was answered almost immediately. The voice was young, male, and all business. "Wethersfield Police, Miz Lawrence. We're going to get you out of there, but we have to break through this siding to do it. Get as far back from the wall as you can, and cover your head and face."

The shock of being answered changed quickly to relief and concern for the officers outside.

"It's Mort Delahanty," I yelled through the crack. "He's crazy. He set the Law Barn on fire," I added unnecessarily as I heard the wail of fire engines rapidly approaching.

"Momma!" Emma yelled from farther away. "Just do it. Do what he says!"

I scrambled to obey and hunkered down against the far wall with my arms over my head. "Okay, I'm away from the wall."

Immediately, the siding was battered by what sounded like a platoon of axes, and I was cheered by the sound of old wood cracking and yielding. Within moments, a large hand reached through the hole that had been created and tore away the jagged planking. I put down my arms and looked up to see Officer Ron Chapman crashing through the man-sized opening, followed closely by Rick Fletcher. The grim expressions on both young men's faces relaxed when they spotted me huddled against the far wall, and I felt tears welling alarmingly.

"Well, hello again, Miz Lawrence," Rick said, handing his axe to Ron and crouching down beside me. His kind young eyes searched my face. "My partner here got the idea that you might be having kind of a rough day, so we thought we'd come and see if we could help you out." From behind him came a cacophony of voices and machines engaged in crowd control and fire fighting. Having correctly assessed my condition as shaky but functional, he stood up and held out a steadying arm as he had only days before on the sidewalk in front of Blades.

I tried to thank Rick but couldn't seem to force words through my suddenly chattering teeth as once again, he hauled me to my feet. I stood for a moment, swaying uncertainly. "Delahanty?" was all I managed to get out.

Ron Chapman spoke up. "Got away from us in the crowd," he said tersely, "but don't worry. There's an all points bulletin out for that black Trans Am. We'll get him." He stepped through the hole in the wall and vanished into the confusion outside.

Rick guided me to the opening and placed a sheltering hand over my head as I eased through the shattered planking. Once again, I found myself the center of attention at a crime scene. "We've got to stop meeting like this," I observed in a feeble attempt at humor. "How did you know where to find me? Over all that noise outside, I'm amazed that anyone could hear me yelling."

"We didn't," Rick grinned. "We knew where you were because we've had you under close surveillance since Glastonbury PD informed us about your little adventure this morning. We knew Delahanty would turn up again, and we didn't want to take any chances. We just didn't figure on your barricading the Law Barn with him inside it. When we couldn't reach you by phone, we figured something must be very wrong in here. We got to Emma, and she knew right away where you'd be hiding. In fact, it was all we could do to keep her from breaking down the wall herself ."

At that moment, Emma herself shoved under the crime scene tape and shook off assorted official hands attempting to restrain her. "Get away from me," she threatened, holding up her hands in a *back off* gesture. "That's my mother, and if I have to drag every last one of you with me, I'm going to her right now." Silent signals passed among the assemblage, and tacit permission was granted to let her through to where I stood awaiting my scrappy daughter. "'Cita?"

Rick turned away discreetly. He really was the nicest young man, I thought again with an inward sigh, but Officer Chapman seemed a decent sort, too. "I'm just fine, Emma, or at least I will be, but I'm afraid I can't say the same for your cell phone. I dropped it on the tiles in there, and…" I held my hands palm up and shrugged bleakly.

"I knew it!" she said. "I knew you'd find some way to destroy my cell phone. I can't believe I trusted you with it. You are so lame." She rolled her eyes and shook her head in mock disgust. Then she hugged me fiercely.

Twelve

In the end, the business association passed a compromise measure that established a limited number of designated, outside smoking areas and banned smoking anywhere else in the historic district. Nobody was completely happy with the measure, but then, as Margo had so correctly pointed out, that's the nature of compromise.

It turned out that Mort Delahanty had served in Viet Nam with Frank Wainwright—had, in fact, saved Frank's life and had the Purple Heart and the post-traumatic stress syndrome to prove it—which is why Frank and Abby gave Mort a job and even shared their home with him for a while, when he fell on hard times years later. Following Frank's death, Mort's gratitude for their kindness had turned into an obsessive need to protect Abby, and when Prudy Crane threatened her well-being, Mort stepped over the edge into madness. He never considered how his chosen method of disposing of Prudy set Abby up for the murder. That realization drove him still further into madness, and, well, we had pretty much figured out the rest.

Ironically, although it had been the entries in her diary that tipped me to Mort, the business with Harriett Wheeler turned out to be of little consequence. Her incessant complaints over several years to the powers that be about Abby's immoral living arrangements had merely earned Harriett the label of eccentric, and thus unworthy of serious attention. In 2002, just before Mort moved into an apartment of his own and bought the infamous Trans Am, Harriett had apparently hired a couple of local teenagers to glue what she felt were appropriate passages from the Bible, condemning adultery and fornication and what have you, to the front door of the Diner, believing that once their customers were aware of the owners' sinfulness, business would drop off sharply. Unfortunately for Harriett, Abby and Frank came to work so early that the public never saw her messages, which they had removed.

"Even if they had," Abby assured me with the first chuckle I had heard from her in a very long time, "they would have rightly attributed it to the work of a crackpot."

I hoped she was right.

Emma never did tell me who she was covering for when she was seen making that blackmail payment to Prudy, and I finally had to accept the fact that she was all grown up now and entitled to her privacy. I let it go, knowing she must have had an awfully good reason for doing what she did. In return, she didn't scold me overly about destroying her cell phone, which I replaced with the very latest model. It does everything but drive for her, but I'm sticking with my faithful little flippy, which the Wethersfield P.D. finally allowed me to retrieve from their evidence locker. She and Ron Chapman seem very well suited to each other, and I enjoy seeing her have some fun with a nice young man, even if it isn't Rick Fletcher. If Emma and Joey have their way, I am never going to hear the end of that one.

The news that the murder charges against Abby Stoddard had been dropped, and Mort Delahanty was sought in connection with the investigation, spread like wildfire. No one has seen him since the night of the hearing, but the dragnet is being tightened in the northwestern Massachusetts area, where Mort apparently has ties to other Viet Nam War veterans. It wouldn't be much longer before he would be apprehended. Despite everything, Abby is anxious that Mort get the help he needs. He saved Frank's life under the worst possible circumstances, and God knows that war messed up the heads of thousands of good men. As Abby put it, "Maybe killing Prudence Crane was an act of sanity, compared with the insanity of being ordered to murder hundreds of innocent civilians," and in that context, I see her point.

The black Trans Am had been parked in the service alley behind the Law Barn, pulled up to the bumper of the Altima, the keys dangling from the ignition. My trunk had been levered open with a crowbar or some such implement. All of the diaries were gone. I didn't miss them.

Margo didn't even want her leather tote bag back and donated it to the Goodwill. She and John Harkness and Rhett Butler were becoming a threesome around town, especially on the weekends when they took long strolls. Abby had taken to stocking a bag of dog cookies behind her counter, and their standard order was "two coffees and a doggie treat to go." I liked the way they looked together.

The fire damage to the Law Barn had been minimal. My assumption about the bonfire on the sofa had been accurate, but I had underestimated the fire retardant qualities of the upholstery, which had stubbornly resisted the flames. When Mort's pile of papers had been consumed, the fire simply died. What damage there was had been caused primarily by smoke and the water trained on the smoldering remains by the firefighters who had been summoned from the station only a block down Old Main Street. As part of the redecorating, we demystified the reading room by adding an actual knob to the door and ditching the big coat rack that had concealed it. We turned the coatroom into a small conference room and now entertain first-time visitors with a tour of the previous owner's eccentricities. I, for one, have had enough of secrets to last me a very long time.

As it turned out, the reading room wasn't all that much of a secret. Any number of locals knew about it, including old Mr. Hitchcock, who came to patch up the exterior wall. He remembered the Viet Nam vet he had taken on "in the summer of '99, I believe it was," at the urging of Frank Wainwright, giving him a few weeks of carpentry and plumbing work on the Picture Palace, his term for the Law Barn during Mr. Watercolors' tenure.

"Fella who owned it then was crazier 'n a bedbug, but hey, work was work. He wanted a secret room, we built him one. It was kinda fun, to tell you the honest truth."

~ * ~

All things considered, I had a lot of news for Strutter, when she finally dragged herself away from her honeymoon, but mostly, I wanted to talk to her about Armando.

"First I was mad, and then I got scared." We were sitting in the late fall sunshine. Strutter's usual attractiveness was unfairly enhanced, I thought meanly, by two weeks of Jamaican frolicking with her new hubby. Charlene "Strutter" Putnam, *nee* Tuttle, was quite simply the most stunning black woman I have ever seen. Soft, brown curls fell to her shoulders, her skin was the color of milk chocolate, and her figure was simultaneously slim and curvaceous. Her warm smile was charmingly framed in dimples.

We occupied one of the four curved benches that surrounded a small fountain to one side of the Keeney Memorial. Although she wasn't due back in the office for another two weeks, I had asked her to meet me for coffee. She hadn't even asked why, just abandoned her honeymoon and showed up an hour later at Ladolce Bakery, where we ordered two cinnamon coffees and took them back out into the glorious morning. Now we sat side by side, faces tilted to the sun, eyes closed. "Mm hmm" had been her only comment thus far. Maybe I hadn't gotten through to her. I opened my eyes and tried again.

"I swear to you, if he had sprouted horns and begun to speak in tongues, I could not have been more astonished. This man, who prides himself on his exquisite courtesy, turns into an arrogant jackass right before my eyes. I'm standing there holding the rake with my mouth hanging open, and he's practically snapping his fingers at an exhausted guy who's been doing heavy labor all day, 'move this', 'rake behind that', like this is his personal servant. 'That's what he gets paid for,' is all he has to offer by way of a rationale. I just wanted to scream at him."

Strutter opened her eyes, which were a startling turquoise color, and took a thoughtful sip of her coffee. "Ooh, that's good. I surely have missed this." She closed her eyes again.

I stared at her, all curls and curves and glowing with honeymoon contentment. With difficulty, I managed not to dump my coffee on her head. "So what do you think," I prompted finally from between gritted teeth, "or perhaps you'd rather I ran along so you can nap in peace?"

Strutter opened her eyes once more and gazed at me with gentle humor.

"Don't get pissy with me, girl, just because your man has fallen off that pedestal you've had him up on. Seems to me that all that's happened here is you've found out you're in love with a real, honest-to-goodness, human-type fella and not God's gift to the human race. And what do I think about that? I think it's about time." Another sip.

"So what should I do?"

"Get over it."

"Get over it? That's your sage advice?"

"You told him how you felt about it. He heard you. Now, move on."

I sat and looked at my good friend for a moment. Strutter had saved my life once. She was maybe the wisest, most centered woman I had ever known, and I loved her like a sister. Maybe more than a sister. At the moment, I wanted to strangle her.

"What superior knowledge gives you the right to tell

me to 'get over it'?"

Strutter grinned. "Ba-dum-bum. It took a little while, but I surely knew it was coming."

I waited some more.

"Okay, here's a little story for you. The week before John and I were married, we planned a sort of a last date. You know, he came over, and I had cooked a romantic little dinner, and he brought flowers and a bottle of wine. Charlie stayed over at a friend's house, so we had the place to ourselves. John built a fire in the fireplace. The whole nine yards."

"Sounds nice. What's your point?"

She chuckled at the memory. "Oh, it was nice. I was on cloud nine, about to be married to the most wonderful man in the world, the whole luxurious evening ahead of us… and then he threw a shoe at my cat."

I was shocked. "John threw a shoe at Farley? He's such a big teddy bear of a cat. I can't imagine it."

"Neither could I, believe me. There I was, putting out my shrimp puffs on the coffee table, ready to snuggle up on the sofa next to my big, sexy man. I was so into the whole thing that I'd forgotten to feed Farley. That's usually Charlie's job. So the poor cat was starving for his dinner, and I plopped a plate of shrimp puffs on the coffee table. He just couldn't help himself. He grabbed one off the plate and ran to the other side of the room to gobble it down and John took off one of his loafers and threw it at him."

"Oh my god, did he hit him?"

"No, he didn't. He swore he had no intention of hitting him, just wanted to scare him and so on and so forth. I lit into him good anyway, of course. But after I stopped yelling and fed the cat, it started to dawn on me that John had no idea why I was upset. He's not an unkind person, you know that, but he wasn't raised with pets, never had a cat or a dog or even a hamster. He was raised on the island, and they have a whole different relationship with critters there. They aren't members of the family like Farley and Jasmine and Simon are. The idea of an animal stealing people's food and being allowed to get away with it was just wrong to him. He has a different perspective, do you see?"

I did see, but I still didn't like it.

"So you got over it."

"I love John, and I always will. Doesn't mean I don't see him clearly. The good news is, I know he loves me the same way, even my less-than-lovable qualities."

"I didn't know you admitted to having any."

Strutter ignored me. "I realize that you're operating under a handicap here."

"Which is?"

"You're a middle-aged white woman who was raised in New England."

"Excuse me?"

She patted my arm apologetically. "I didn't mean that as an ethnic slur or anything."

"Yes, you did."

We were quiet for a moment as Strutter weighed what she still had to say against my ability to hear it. It was a thing I'd seen her do dozens of times. Then she shrugged, and I knew she had decided to say her piece and hope I could take it.

"Housepets are not in John's cultural frame of reference. It's the same with Manny and servants."

"I don't have any servants!"

"Nooo, but in Colombia, I'm sure he did. He was probably brought up with them, and where he comes from, that's how you talk to servants, how his mother and his *tias* talked to them. It's not unkind, really, just authoritarian. It's the way it's done in Latin America."

I had to hand it to her. She had my attention.

"In New England, on a hot day in July, I'll bet your mama brought the guy who mowed your lawn a glass of lemonade or maybe some iced tea, am I right?"

I nodded.

"And you do the same, don't you?"

I nodded again. "Of course I do. It's only civil."

"But you don't have one with him, stand around and chat."

"No. He'd think that was weird."

"Uh huh. He's grateful for the cold drink, but anything more than that would be uncomfortable for both of you. Well, in Jamaica, where I was raised, and probably in Colombia, too, the gardener cools off with a drink from the hose. He's glad to have access to it, but beyond that, he'd just as soon be left alone. That's what he expects, and that's what he's comfortable with. It's his cultural frame of reference."

"But this isn't Colombia."

"So you need to talk to him about how things are done here. He looks fairly trainable to me."

I chewed on that for a while. "So you're saying I overreacted."

She twinkled at me kindly. I had a feeling that Strutter was a very good mom, although I am fully ten years her senior.

"How's married life?" I asked her, changing the subject.

"Married life is just fine, thank you. I think I'll get back to it and let you get back to work."

We stood and hugged briefly.

"Tell Margo I said hey. I'll see you in a couple of weeks."

I watched her walk that walk of hers, the one that had earned Strutter her nickname, across the street to where her little gray Jetta waited patiently in the shade. John Putnam was a lucky fellow, I thought, not for the first time.

Then I pulled my cell phone out of my handbag and called Manny.

Meet Judith K. Ivie

A Connecticut native, Judith K. Ivie has been a working writer and editor for more than 25 years. Her previous "day jobs" ran the gamut of communications and public relations positions, including investor relations and editing a high-tech periodical for architects and engineers. She is currently executive assistant to a corporate president and CEO.

Along the way Judith also published three full-length nonfiction books and many articles focusing on workplace issues. Second editions of her earlier books, *Calling It Quits: Turning Career Setbacks to Success*, and *Working It Out: The Domestic Double Standard* were published by Whiskey Creek Press in 2005 and 2006.

Recently, she has added fiction to her repertoire. Her first mystery and a romance novel were published in 2006 by Wings Press, and she has just completed a second mystery.

**VISIT OUR WEBSITE
FOR THE FULL INVENTORY
OF QUALITY BOOKS**:

http://www.wings-press.com

*Quality trade paperbacks and downloads
in multiple formats,
in genres ranging from light romantic comedy to
general fiction and horror. Wings has something
for every reader's taste.
Visit the website, then bookmark it.
We add new titles each month!*